MW01599134

and me among them

and me among them
Kristen den Hartog

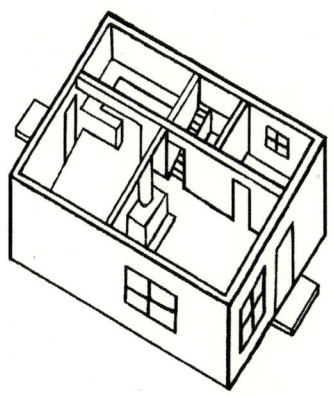

a novel

Freehand Books gratefully acknowledges the support of the Canada Council for the Arts for its publishing program. ¶ Freehand Books, an imprint of Broadview Press Inc., gratefully acknowledges the financial support for its publishing program provided by the Government of Canada through the Canada Book Fund.

Canada Council   Conseil des Arts
for the Arts   du Canada

Freehand Books
412−815 1st Street SW   Calgary, Alberta   T2P 1N3
www.freehand-books.com

Book orders: Broadview Press Inc.
280 Perry Street, Unit 5   Peterborough, Ontario   K9J 2J4
Telephone: 705-743-8990 Fax: 705-743-8353
customerservice@broadviewpress.com
www.broadviewpress.com

Library and Archives Canada Cataloguing In Publication

Den Hartog, Kristen, 1965−
And me among them / Kristen den Hartog.

ISBN 978-1-55481-054-3

     I. Title.

PS8557.E537A64 2011   C813'.6   C2011-900544-1

Edited by Robyn Read
Book design by Natalie Olsen, Kisscut Design
Author photo by Jeff Winch

Printed on FSC recycled paper and bound in Canada

For Nellie

Even after I have reached the pinnacle of my growth, I still find safety in my yellow room, a museum holding the souvenirs of my existence. My collections of pine cones and pressed leaves are here, as are the stacks of tattered comic books I've read a hundred times. There are miniature soldiers as well, salvaged from my father's childhood and passed from him to me. Feet molded to tiny platforms, they wield weapons and bugles, and stand at attention as I rise up, up, pushing right through the roof to look down on the little world below.

I can see out, all the way to far-off lands, and I can see back, to years and years ago; place and time unravels in all directions. My eyes and ears are many times the size they should be. My heart is swollen. My bones are weak. But something good can come from even the most terrifying things. For everything that is taken away, something else is given.

So here I am, head in the clouds. Family photographs resting in my huge hands. I hold the pictures by their edges, the way I was shown to as a little girl, and I see me and my mother and father locked into the grains of silver. My thumb can obliterate a house or a row of people, so I take great care as I crack open the flat, drab photographs to release us all in a spill of colour.

First to come is my father James. I hover over him as he makes his way through town on his postal route, and along the way I see Elspeth, my mother, deposited at the suit factory, reaching for the sewing machine in front of her. Her brown hair curves around her ears and is smooth and glossy, trimmed to perfection. Her skin is pale but flushed at the cheeks and her lips are fuller than usual. Pregnancy softens her, but she has always been pretty in her quiet, delicate way. The big belly that contains me is covered by a dress she made herself, white with yellow swirls. Later she will undo the stitches and refashion it to fit her slender frame, but for now the belly beneath comes between her and her work, and I feel the hard ridge of the machine press against my forming body. The vibration as it pulls the cloth through is my clue to the outside world, like the hum of her voice, or the sound of James whispering each night, telling me how things will be. But nothing prepares me, or any of us, for what's to come.

Elspeth quits her job at the suit factory weeks before I am born, when her stomach gets in the way of her arms reaching the machine. Everyone says she has to be further along than she thinks she is, or that there are two babies inside of her rather than just me. Is it because she is small, or because I'm big? Already we are defined by each other, and we haven't even met yet. We haven't looked at each other or touched on the outside. Thinking of it this way, the fact that I'm growing inside her body seems like an invasion of privacy. Hers and my own.

I watch as the other seamstresses throw a party for Elspeth on her last day. Someone brings a three-tiered cake dripping with icing, with a china baby on top surrounded by sugared violets. Sitting in the quiet factory that normally whirs with the sound of machines, Elspeth looks at the figurine—his fixed gaze and his menacing smile. She insists someone else cut the cake, but then she is given the piece with the baby stuck to it, and he stares up at her as the sweet taste fills her mouth. She has never liked sweet things.

She begins to see out her pregnancy in the ordinary ways, readying the very room I'm in now and napping in the afternoons. She paints the walls bright yellow, which is not a popular colour nor one she particularly likes, but something compels her to do it. Me, perhaps, pushing a wish through the umbilical cord. Every day James comes home from his postal route and says he wishes she would wait and let him do the painting, but she can't possibly wait. She is nesting, or panicking. She climbs up and down the ladder and pushes herself to exhaustion with the need for everything to be just so. I am an honoured guest due to arrive at any moment. All of my things await me in their appropriate places, and

11

in this room, where Elspeth often sits in silence, an aura of anticipation rises, yellow as the sun, around which everything revolves.

The women at the factory have used their various skills to fashion sleepers and booties for me, as well as little hats and underthings. One woman—Iris—embroidered the flower of her name onto a bib, which to Elspeth seems a strangely personal thing to do, given that Iris is nothing more than a co-worker. More clothes and blankets have come from my grandmother, who saved everything from James's infancy. Elspeth folds the linens into dresser drawers scented with lavender sachets. But as the pregnancy progresses, it seems unlikely that I will fit into such tiny garments.

Day by day I turn in Elspeth's womb, a dark, shadowy place with an orange glow. My ears prick when James sings to me, and I sit still, hugging my legs and listening, sensing his presence outside. The orange glow dissipates when he comes close and puts his ear to Elspeth's belly, and then seeps in again when he moves away. I put my hand out to him, and he sees it moving under her skin, presses his own palm against it.

My time is coming closer. Elspeth's stomach stretches further and rings of purple discolour her ankles. She is bedridden in the days leading up to my birth, and James brings her meals on a tray and eats next to her, propping her up with pillows. But her appetite is waning. There is no room in the overextended stomach that bulges beneath her nightgown. The heartburn, she says, is unbearable, and she has to sleep sitting up, which means that the weight presses on her bladder, and she feels a constant need to pee. Her toes are cold and James has to put her slippers on for her because she can't reach that far herself. In the hard line of her jaw, in the frantic shifting of her bloodshot eyes, he sees an anxiety caused by something other than physical discomfort, and he waits for her to confess a wash of fears that would be lessened by the simple fact of her head on his chest, the drum of his heart beneath her ear, as always. That is his role, the soother, but she doesn't ask to be soothed, and he is unsure how to behave when nothing has been requested of him. At times in his life he's known this to be his weakest trait.

While convinced she is as terrified as he, James doesn't offer his own fears for discussion, or explain his irrational panic when, between Monday and Tuesday in the middle of the night, he hears the doorbell ring. It rings once in his sleep to awaken him, and then again as he rises on his elbows in bed, blinking. He looks at Elspeth, whose face, inches from his own, is still as death. As he is sometimes moved to do, he puts his hand in front of her mouth to satisfy himself that she is breathing. In his slippers he steps through the dark house, stands in the hall, and places one eye close to the door's window.

"James, what are you doing?"

Her voice startles him and sends a shock up the back of his neck and over his scalp. He turns toward her and sees her standing in a column of light that comes through the window. Her hands clasp her big stomach, and he watches my foot travel across the width of her, masked by clothes and skin.

"Did you hear the doorbell?" he asks.

"No. I heard you."

He puts a finger to his lips and opens the door. A leaf scuttles across the walk. The sailboat chimes tinkle in the

13

breeze, and then slow to nothing. Under the yellow porch light, the pavement glistens with dew.

"Come to bed," she tells him wearily. "You were dreaming."

And beside her his heart aches in the darkness. He keeps his eyes shut and lets his mouth fall open in case she's watching him. He even fakes a snore rattling at the back of his throat, and rolls away from her to face the wall. But he remains awake, waiting.

Later James will tell me I was born with manners—*you rang the doorbell first, and then we asked you in*—and he'll pass over the other details of the night and morning: the gush of water breaking, Elspeth squatting in the tub and him in there with her, stroking her hair and feeling altogether useless in underwear and bare feet. She clings so tightly to his legs he thinks his bones are crushing. As he watches her moan through the contractions, a deep animal sound that echoes throughout the neighbourhood, he feels almost afraid of her power. For it is she, holding him so tightly, who keeps both of them from slipping down the drain in a black spiral. This is an emergency—he should have known. Her eyes roll back in her head, and red veins creep across the whites. She has to tell him, "Call an ambulance," and he lays her down in the tub and runs to the phone.

Even in the hospital she believes what is happening to her has never happened to anyone else before. As they wheel her away, she looks at James and sees the fear in his eyes and knows she can't say what she's thinking: *we're dying. The baby and I will both die together.*

But her silent frenzy subsides as the anaesthetic pulses through her. It rushes along this vein and that to ensure tranquility, and she feels herself smiling and rising to another place. There is no such peace for me. I come shuddering through a hole too small for me, fighting to stay inside of Elspeth while every part of me is squeezed and shoved forward. Forceps clamp my head and pull me. Light burns my eyes, sounds scrape my eardrums, and the cold air pierces through me. The cord that joins us is cut, and though it was part of both of our bodies, neither of us feels it happen. I am washed and bundled by strangers who record the first details about me as Elspeth sleeps. In a way she isn't present when I am born, even further off than James who roams the hospital halls with his shirt crookedly buttoned, his socks mismatched, his mind travelling to other bone-chilling events as a way of convincing himself he can get through this one too. Until a nurse taps his shoulder.

"Mr. Brennan," she says. "Congratulations. You have a healthy baby girl."

In the autumn of 1947, I weighed eight pounds, two ounces. Everything about me was normal, James had been told this, but he felt relieved that he could see it from the doorway, where he stood grinning foolishly with a spray of carnations in his hand. Elspeth held on to me, beaming and staring out the window. My milky, brand new eyes followed, as if I was searching for someone out there. James inched forward and sat beside us, perched on the edge of the bed. When Elspeth turned toward him, he pressed his forehead to hers, so they formed a kind of temple over me, a position that looked like a promise from each side but was only two tired people resting. James said, "She's beautiful," and Elspeth agreed. But that was just what everyone said about all babies.

They named me Ruth Frances Beatrice Brennan, and took me home. The days blended together, one into another with no distinctions. The crying, the feeding, the changing, the chafing, the washing, the soothing, the burping, the singing, the sleeping, the waking. As new parents, James and Elspeth were surprised by their fatigue, as well as my dismissal of it. If someone had told them what to expect (and no one had), they hadn't taken it in, and now, rather than forging ahead, they were rolling and rolling.

Sometimes Elspeth hung over me with smears of purple under her eyes, the skin there loose and fine, like something that would tear easily. She begged me to understand, though she knew she asked too much of me. Just as I asked too much of her, and him, and they of each other. James formed a habit of going to get things before they were needed, because it made him feel helpful and also allowed him to escape, just briefly, what he'd never expected to have to endure.

Soon, ghouls and monsters came to the door, demanding candy. They stood on the step while the wind moaned behind them, and Elspeth dropped sweets into open pillowcases, imagining me and all the things I'd be on future Halloweens. Eyes darted behind homemade masks. All evening the creatures came and went with the wind. Their capes and gowns whipped around their bodies, and a witch's hat flew by with no witch beneath it. James relit the grinning jack-o'-lantern each time the wind extinguished it, but sometime after midnight Elspeth parted the curtains and saw it in the road, smashed to pieces. No matter. It had disturbed her more when it sat glowing on the porch, nose, eyes, mouth eroded, like a real face rotting away. She let the curtains fall closed and walked back to her chair, *clip-clop*. In those early days, she wore her shoes until bedtime; James wore his tie. There was something formal about both of them, in their individual ways and their interactions as a couple, while there was something primal about me, the thing they'd made together.

The autumn wind continued as Elspeth fed me from one breast and then the other, and watched my jaw working as I sucked each of them empty. For much of my life to come I'd be hungry, dying of thirst. I looked up at her as though I'd really begun to see her, as though I'd already discovered *if I can see you, you can see me*, and while I waited for her to speak, she sang a song about rivers, and stroked the rim of my ear, up, down, up, down. My ears were almost see-through. She could place her fingers behind them and see them moving, as with the fine porcelain tea set she'd brought from England, with its rosette pattern that her mother had picked for her own married life. Things go back and back, just as they go forward.

When she finished her song, I rested in my playpen, peering through the bars and observing her as she went about her tasks. Sometimes, the watch shifted; as I lay sleeping in the bassinette she'd trimmed with ribbon and lace before I was born, she sat looking at me, unable to believe I had come, that loving me was so easy and such a burden right at the same time. She couldn't just sit and love me, she had to do the countless things that proved it to be true, and she had to keep on doing them, hour after hour. With every day that passed, she felt a little more of herself disappear, and it reminded her of when she'd come to James by ship, getting further and further from England and leaving everything she knew of herself behind.

Outside, in the first winter of my life, the trees stood like black skeletons and the snow came and smothered everything. Icicles hung in glittering clusters from the eavestroughs, and my eyes turned a clear, deep blue. Every day I could see further away, with greater clarity, but the mysteries of being alive multiplied. Elspeth, an English war bride, hated Canadian winters, and any sign of her discomfort made James tend the wood stove too faithfully, so the house was overly warm and I passed my days in a fog of lethargy. Eyelids heavy, limbs of rubber. Elspeth took care of my every need, combing the wisps of my hair with her fingers. Such a peaceful feeling. There was a silence to those early years, as if we were all three contained in a bubble each knew would burst, and we were savouring this sacred time given to us.

At first I was a squalling new baby, carried from room to room, with no power of my own. But I was growing. Soon, in my high chair, I pierced wild blueberries with one tooth and sucked out the contents, spitting the skins onto the tray. As I took my first steps in stiff, white shoes, my big feet gave me a puppyish look. By two I was surprisingly articulate, and began to introduce myself to other children at the playground.

"Hello," I said, sidling up to a girl with clips in her tufts of hair. I curled an arm around her little shoulders and pressed my face close to hers. "I'm Roof." *Blink-blink.* "What does *your* name?"

The little face across from mine stared in wonder. The mouth went O, and I moved to the next child.

"What does *your* name?"

Wasn't it strange how no one would answer? The vacant expression on each new face, the wide, drifting eyes, and the swings swinging in the background. I wandered from child to child, and no one knew what to make of me. The playground was its own world, with green grass stretching on forever, and a sandbox that kept unearthing treasures the deeper you dug. But none of it held me the way a child's face did. Whenever I saw children I wanted to grab their small hands in mine and squeeze, and pull the little people around with me.

I was already different. But there was nothing wrong with me yet—there was nothing bad. Elspeth and James mimicked my funny expressions, the way I called myself *Roof,* and my enduring ability to turn everything into a question.

"See, Ruthie," said James, "the leaves are falling."

"Why, Daddy?"

"Well. Because the trees are going to sleep."

"Why are they going to sleep?"

"Because they're tired from growing all summer."

"But why?"

"Why what, Ruthie? Why do they grow?"

"Why do they grow in summer?"

"Well, because that's when it's warm."

"Why is it warm in summer?"

"Because that's when our part of the earth is closer to the sun. See up there?"

21

We craned our necks.

"The sun," I said, squinting.

"Right."

"Why is it yellow?"

"It's a big ball of fire in the sky. Yellowy-orange fire."

"Why doesn't the fire go out when it rains? Why?"

"I guess because the sun is higher up than the rain clouds. It's further away."

"But Dad."

"Hmm, Ruthie?"

"Why?"

On it went. He was floored by how much he didn't know —the very basics of life on earth—and how much he might learn by raising me.

Photographs from this time show the possibility in my little girl's face, and Elspeth becoming less happy as the years went by. By the age of four I began to look foolish in the frilly dresses Elspeth stitched on her sewing machine, one every few weeks since I outgrew them so quickly. My rubber boots were the size of a seven-year-old's, but I loved how they took me through puddles to the shores of a distant land. There were trees that talked, and flowers that grew taller than me, and roads of yellow brick as in the Land of Oz. This was a place I escaped to again and again, and I wished, sometimes, that I could take Elspeth with me, but when I tried to imagine her there I saw her as she had become in her ordinary world, with her worried expression, her whispered prayers that came on suddenly and filled me with fear. I knew (though the guilt from it ached in me) that the place would wither upon her arrival. No, I didn't want her in my secret land.

Instead I took her dressmaker's dummy, the sleek, brown form that had come with her from England. The dummy had a lovely, gentle shape, and could be wheeled from room to room along the roads of my imagination. It would be years until I tired of her, until I understood that the downfall of imagination is that it always, always ends. I tied a ribbon to her wire skirt, and slipped with her behind the curtains the day King George VI died. Elspeth wept into the laundry, scrubbing stains with the hard bristles of a dangerous brush. Crying for something that felt like my fault, though I'd never known King George or any other king in my lifetime. For Elspeth's sake, I wished I could revive him. At Christmas, I'd gotten a dollhouse complete with gingerbread trim and miniature people, and now I made it George's house, his country house, and peered at the royal family through the windows, reaching in with my big fingers to move them from room to room. When I stared long enough at the faces with their painted expressions, I got a scary feeling that the dolls were becoming real right before my eyes. I was staring them into being. It didn't matter that I was many times their size; they still frightened me, so I pinched the curtains closed to keep them from seeing me, and tucked the house away for another day.

The doctor laughed when he saw me next.

"Well, there seems to be no stopping Ruth Brennan!" He dismissed my aches as growing pains, though he gave me several sideways glances.

Elspeth didn't believe him, but she wanted to. James simply wished everything would be okay, that someone who knew things would tell them so. Clusters of hair sprang from the doctor's ears, and it was perhaps these that kept

23

him from thinking clearly and diagnosing my condition.

"Is there anyone else exceptionally tall?" he asked. "In the family, I mean?"

James thought of his stocky parents and his brother Norm, five-six with sloping shoulders. "No, not really," he answered. "Well, a cousin, I think, on my grandpa's side. Or a cousin twice removed?"

Great Gregory, they called him, a rodeo star. Great Gregory could ride his bucking bronco for so long without being thrown off that the horse would eventually sink to the ground with exhaustion, and Great Gregory would scoop him up and let him ride on his massive shoulders eating feathery oats until a second wind came.

On Elspeth's side, two mannish aunties, Franny and Bea, soared in unison to at least six-foot-four. She'd told me herself. Their names were my middle names, but no, sorry, there were no pictures. The aunts lived in England, and I always pictured them as Gog and Magog from a book we had about England's medieval parades. Two wicker giants with old sheets for clothing and frizzed, tinselly hair. Fierce guardians of the city of London, they'd paraded in the Lord Mayor's Show since the days of King Henry v. To make the people wonder, they were set forth in all their ugliness, marching as if alive, wielding swords and shields, but within they were stuffed with nothing more than paper and straw. The Great Fire gobbled them, but Gog and Magog, like all the best giants, could be made and remade—of wicker, of wood, of legend. Time and again they would fall victim to the small but ruthless mice that chewed away at them, or to mould, floods, the Blitz. And time and again they would rise up to guard once more.

Our town was cut in two by a river. Three bridges hinged the halves together; Elspeth said these looked like toys compared to the more grand bridges that stretched over the Thames in London. Our house was one of many in a residential neighbourhood at the east end of town. Where the streets ended lay a meadow fringed by forest, and, in front of that, a secluded, marshy beach. The public beach was on the opposite side of the river, along with tidy neighbourhoods that mirrored ours. A road curved along either bank, like two lines drawn to keep the town from slipping down into the water. The buildings of downtown—the shops, the town council offices, the fire station, the police station—sat facing each other, with the river between, and further on from them stood the school, a series of churches, the factory where Elspeth had worked, and finally the pulp and paper mill.

James's mail route took him down toward the water several times and back up again through the quiet streets. Every day he delivered good news and bad into the mouths of houses. Lifting the lips, he slid the letters in. He wore a sharp, blue uniform and kept his heavy bag strapped over his torso. It grew lighter as the day wore on, and his step quickened with the pleasant notion of burdens falling away. The route was his chance to order his world. As he walked, he thought about me and my awkward, gangly way of moving. I looked like a marionette on invisible strings, my wayward limbs drifting out from me. He told himself that I'd had a head start, as the doctor had suggested, and that soon I'd slow down and become normal. A little larger than normal, but it was true that the human race was growing in stature, and he'd read that tall people do well in life, better than short ones. He was five-foot-nine, bigger than his brother Norm, but during the war it had not been lost on him that his superiors really were tall men, for the most part, with broad shoulders. Which wasn't to say that he'd envied them or had wanted to be different. He was actually quite content, even thankful. He remembered waiting for the ship that would bring Elspeth, along with hundreds of other brides, and how he'd first spotted her in the crowd, coming down the ramp toward him, bringing a merciful ending to the most violent chapter of his life and hers: a time when he'd killed and nearly been killed himself; a time of enormous loss for her.

But if he was happy, or able to tell himself he was, she was less so. After all, she'd left everything behind: a neighbourhood still digging itself out of the rubble, a church whose steeple had split in two, the graves of loved ones, and a little hat shop that had passed through generations and come through the war (like her) physically unscathed. And now, in return, there was me.

As I got taller, Elspeth dreamed that she'd woken up during my birth and had tried to push me back into herself. The pressure sent my blood coursing through me like a poison. My legs grew bone-thin with huge knees, and my arms bulged at the elbows. The dreams came and went, and if she woke crying in the night, James held her until she slept again—was actually thankful for the nightmares because they made him feel useful, and got her reaching for him. Each morning she woke curled into him with a fresh hopefulness, a kind of blank slate, until the realities of her days came through to her again. And she looked at him as he slept, and wondered what her life might be like if she had never come to this place where the blandness of her surroundings was inescapable, and people spoke too slowly and smiled too much with their big, white teeth. What would her life be like if she and James had never met?

There almost had been someone else. Richard Wilson, tall, with beautiful eyes. He was so charismatic that even streetwise cats ran to catch up with him on the sidewalk. There in front of the hat shop, they rolled over in front of him and asked to have their matted bellies scratched, and he smiled, complied for a moment or two, and carried on his way.

※

By five I had a snarl of black curly hair and my blue eyes were round as buttons, as if everything that passed before them surprised me. Which wasn't true. I already knew that things unfolded a certain way no matter how hard I wished, and that God wasn't someone you asked for things.

But I lit up in the presence of boys and girls. I could happily play alone at the beach if the other children were close by. In the sun making castles, I transformed a piece of bark into a bridge just by placing it within the frame. A twig with a leaf at its tip grew into a flagpole, and my finger dug a watery moat wide enough to keep the enemy at bay. This game I could play all day unless the laughter of the children drew me in. Then I lumbered after them, barely noticing my size as sand sprayed behind my feet, and my overlong arms and legs flailed clumsily. I flopped on top of a girl to capture her the way a normal child catches a frog or a mouse.

27

The girl pinned beneath me screamed a scream that vibrated in my own body. How I loved that closeness! The smell of skin and hair in my nostrils. But then the dark shadow of Elspeth enveloped me, and her hands clasped my armpits and pulled me up from the child whose smooth skin was dotted with sand.

The girl scrambled out from beneath me. Laughter was barking out of me when the girl turned and said in a serious voice, "Can you stop chasing us please? We just don't want to play with you." I swallowed and nodded, hot all over. I felt Elspeth watching, hearing every word.

Her hand squeezed mine as we returned to our towels, and neither of us spoke as she brushed the sand from my feet and folded the towels corner to corner. She took me home in the car with the wasted sun still shining, the summer day barely begun. The car's wheels hummed over the riverside road, and I felt the rumble of the bridge beneath us as we crossed the water. The hum again, turning homeward. The whole way I looked out the side window at the trees rushing past, and the houses, my giant face superimposed upon them.

The questions I asked as a little girl had an effect on James even when we weren't together. As he walked his mail route, he pondered the mysteries of ordinary things such as the structure of houses, and how it had come to be that four walls and a roof sheltered people. He thought about every detail, including the hinges that held the doors on and the windows that brought in or shut out the world, depending.

He thought about the foundation of a house, which couldn't be seen but was the tough, deep root of an otherwise precarious structure. Since the average ceiling was eight feet high and a door was less than seven, he imagined that I would one day grow past both those heights, up through the ceiling, the snapping rafters, the roof, and that I was certain to ask him, "Daddy, what if I never stop growing?" And he would have to answer, because he'd always answered. He prided himself on that. What would he say?

That's impossible, Ruthie.

But was it? He pictured the roof tiles lifting up into the sky like birds flying, and then he shook his head and focused again on the doorknobs, the hinges, and his own sure steps on the sidewalk.

He believed happiness was a matter of conviction, so he sometimes whistled, but such buoyancy was wearing. There were days when the weight of his bag of letters became unbearable, and his uniform, the navy pants and jacket, felt as though it had been dipped in lead. And then it reminded him of his soldier's uniform, heavy with wet mud and stinking of war, and that deepened the heaviness, which came on slowly until it overcame him. To lift his foot, an ordinary foot, was to lift the foot of a giant. If he opened his mouth and let his voice out, he felt certain it would be a baritone voice, but so slowed and distorted that the words would be meaningless.

As he expanded out and up, he looked down on the trees and the pattern of houses that formed his route, and a teardrop fell and made a lake in an empty field. He tried to put his foot down, but everywhere he looked there was something he might step on. Little people went by on bicycles, and a lost deer hurried over his shoe, thinking it part of the landscape. *Get out of the way,* he bellowed, but the words stretched and droned like a strong wind. He was so far away. Perhaps no one could hear him; but at least they couldn't be frightened if they didn't know of his presence. He put his huge hands to his huge face and covered it, just as a child would do, believing that if he couldn't see, he would also not be seen.

When he took his hands away, he was small again, standing on the sidewalk to his own home. For a long moment he stared at the house, its white stucco exterior blazing in the sun.

Close an eye and encircle the open one with your thumb and finger, and through that lens you can see the fine details of your kneecap or your hand. See how the skin is woven like fabric, spun from many things? Or hold the lens up and look far, so far off you can see mountains, where a little house is nestled with smoke puffing out of the chimney. You can see great distances through a thumb-and-finger telescope. Try it.

I had always wanted to tell someone that. Not Elspeth or James, but a child like me. And once I started school that chance would be there. As the day came closer, I thought about how I'd stand in front of the class and tell them what I knew. But then I pictured myself displayed in front of the other students, all of them watching me, and my heart beat so loud that I knew it would drown out my words. I would open my mouth and nothing but the *knock-knock* sound would come out, and everyone would laugh. Before I even got to school, my ease around other children eroded, the way a bone erodes and can never grow strong again.

On my first day, I was creeping up on five feet, heads taller than my peers, who stared at me as I made my way down the speckled hall to my classroom, sweaty hand gripping Elspeth's sleeve. *Clip-clop* went Elspeth's shoes, and her dark dress without a speck of lint swished against her nylons, like people whispering. Elspeth was slim and dark-haired with a natural elegance. In Canada, her English accent gave her a level of sophistication that wasn't earned, for she'd had little education and was far from worldly. But she looked the part. She used a steel blue pencil to trace the edges of her brown eyes, and dusted the fine bones of her face with bronze powder. I wished that one day I'd be like her. Letting go of her sleeve and entering Room 7 made me feel like a balloon released into the sky, and I kept looking to the window to see if she'd appear there with James behind her. If necessary I could climb through to them and we could all escape together, running from the teacher's long reach, a hand with claws and grotesque knuckles.

But no, the teacher was nothing like that. I faced front, and saw her smiling straight at me. Frizzy silver hair like aunties Gog and Magog. I thought, *Maybe I could love it here.* The hum of the fluorescent lights, the alphabet travelling around the classroom perimeter. She told us we could do great things with our lives—even the girls—and whether or not it was true, I liked to hear her think up different possibilities of who we could be each time she pointed to the letters: an architect, a botanist, a cartographer, a dancer, an equestrian, a friend, a geologist, a husband, an ice skater, a jockey, a kindergarten teacher, a lumberjack, a musician, a neuro-surgeon, an Olympian, a philosopher, a quilt maker, a rodeo rider, a scientist, a taxidermist, an undertaker, a veterinarian, a wife, a xylophonist, a Yeoman of the Guard, a zoologist.

When at recess a boy put on my coat and ran back and forth with my long sleeves flapping, the teacher sent him to a corner and made him stay there until class resumed. I thought I had an ally then, but once everyone was seated again she made him come to me and apologize.

"Say sorry to Ruth," she said as the class looked on.

I turned away from the boy's face, from the spots of red on his cheeks and the humiliation in his eyes that branded me as his enemy. As he spoke a mocking "soar-reee," I looked at my sock bunched down around my ankle, my long foot toe to toe with his.

"It's okay," I told him, but really the opposite was true. He, and the others watching, were lost to me for good.

So why was it that I was happy to be among them? I took their company in whatever form it came, just as a starving person eats whatever she finds. I was put at the back of the class so I wouldn't obscure the view of the other children, and I found myself grinning at the funny way the teacher's arm jiggled when she wrote with chalk on the board; at the bee doing a loop-dee-loop outside the window, threatening to fly in. I gripped my pencil, but against my will it snuck up to my face and made a curly moustache on my upper lip. Curls and more curls, the delicious lead-wood smell, and the sharp tip of the pencil tickling my skin. Waiting for the others to turn to me was almost more than I could bear, and my eyes grazed fondly from one child to the next. The funny boy with the ring of dirt around his neck. The cross-eyed girl with braids and corrective glasses. Grace was her name.

Grace seemed almost like a friend, though we'd never spoken directly. I tried to predict what she might think was funny and curled my top lip up to hold my pencil there. I crossed my eyes for her and plugged my ears with erasers. At recess my heart thumped with the thought of going close to her, but she could see me coming, even when I approached from behind. Maybe her glasses gave her special spin-around vision? It was as though we held an invisible, unbendable pole between us, for whenever I moved close, she moved just that distance away. Little shoulders, little ears, little ski jump nose. I put my hand out from yards away and pretended to stroke her hair.

I stood alone in the playground as the swings flew and the monkey bars filled up with children. My hands reached almost to my knees; I was all wrong, out of proportion. I listened to the hiss of the pulp and paper mill across the river, to the whir of the factory where Elspeth had worked. The wind hugged me. It made whispering sounds, circled my feet with a trailing of sand, then spiralled around me, up, up, until I was reeling. If I closed my eyes the children's voices faded and all I could hear was the whistling of the atmosphere, someone far off calling me. It was a spooky sound, but reassuring too: somewhere, someone knew me and was waiting for me to come.

At home after school I liked to sit on the floor and draw pictures of me with Elspeth and James in front of our house, and a yellow sun in the right-hand corner with lines I called "the shine" coming out. I drew Grace too, with her braids and glasses. There were always fingerprints on her lenses, and I wanted to tell her how you could breathe on them and then rub the fog away with something soft and unscratchy.

"Mum, how do you draw people the way they really look?" I asked Elspeth. "When will I be able to?"

She answered, "In time, with practice, if you keep at it enough," but there was a kernel of doubt inside me, and I knew it was there inside her as well. Why could I *see* just how people looked but not convey it? I felt there must be some clue, some trick—a secret withheld from me—and sometimes I scribbled in hot frustration, ripping through the paper to the floor beneath. I could still kneel easily enough and hunch over my work the way any child would; I had no idea that one day the position would be unthinkable for me. My awkwardness showed more in the way I concentrated, with my tongue stuck out of the left side of my mouth. I held my pencil incorrectly, between my third and fourth fingers. And there were other mistakes too; the things I hadn't noticed about myself my giant ears overheard.

"All these strange little flaws," said Elspeth. "Where do they come from?"

"Those things aren't flaws," said James. "They're quirks. Everyone has quirks. You're pigeon-toed." This last he spoke with a sneer.

Elspeth didn't respond, but thought, *Pigeons don't have toes, not really.* In her view, a cluster of flaws had shown up in James, too. His happy-go-lucky simple-mindedness. His

35

mouth, which reeked of coffee until a sour smell took over late in the day. She noticed a change in his tone when he spoke of her toes—un-James, she thought, and spiteful. Sign of a widening rift. Elspeth had begun to see cracks in the bedroom walls, and the walls in the kitchen and living room as well. There were places where the plaster bulged, pulling away from the lath. And she heard sounds, late at night but also in the daytime when she was alone in the house. The walls cracked and breathed. Houses could fall apart in moments—the war had taught her that—so it was true that it could happen over time as well, with the people trapped inside. When she put her hand next to the fault lines, the air emerging felt warm and moist, like human breath. All day she listened. She listened after the clothes had been washed and dried, while she was folding them. She listened after the floor had been polished, while she was observing the gleam. Not admiring her work exactly but registering it as a task completed. She scrubbed the house until her skin stung and her nostrils tingled from the sharp chemical fumes. But she never managed to achieve that same sense of accomplishment she'd had at the hat shop in England, or even at the factory, sewing pocket after pocket for the suits of businessmen. Longing for that monotonous piecework, followed by a more pervasive longing for home, for England, brought her close to crying. She remembered the little church in her neighbourhood that had split in two and regretted that she was not going to church often enough. Maybe God was taking revenge. Her whispered prayers were not enough of an allegiance. One day she dug out a plaque of praying hands from among her English mementoes. She nailed it to the wall in the hallway. Though the hands gave her some comfort, they frightened me. I sometimes thought of them as I was falling asleep—hands with no body, reaching for me, and me alone in the dark. Elspeth and James, at least, had each other. At the end of each day, after I'd been tucked into my own bed, James pulled Elspeth close, and she welcomed the ritual embrace.

I love you, he said.

I love you too, she said.

There were nights when the words were like a warning, to remind each of the other's expectations. And then at times they were spoken with a wistful expression, heads tipped to the side as if exchanging an apology.

I kept drawing. My pictures took on an ancient Egyptian look, though I knew little of that era; I often drew faces in profile but with the eye staring straight out, and the torso beneath it turned forward. Trees were drawn from the side, but ponds from above, as though I'd flown past, looking down on them. I sat on the floor and drew for hours on end, and when I noticed my tongue sticking out, I pulled it in and made a silent promise to better myself. In pictures I didn't embellish. I didn't draw things I'd never seen. I drew Elspeth, James, and myself, and I labelled us Mum, Dad, Me, though there was no mistaking who was whom. The depictions were crude yet honest. The mother had her hair pulled back and if I drew her full face, I placed the number 11 between her eyebrows.

"What's this?" she asked.

I reached out and touched the worry lines on her face.

37

"That's your double scar," I said.

She smiled, or appeared to. She was twenty-nine years old.

James wore a happier expression. I drew him in his mail suit and cap, and the big bag strapped over his torso made him shorter on one side than the other, just as it did in real life. His mouth was squeezed into an O, and I pointed to that and said, "He's whistling," then attempted to whistle too. My lips puckered in my big face, but no sound came out.

"No, like this, Ruth," said Elspeth, and she whistled the tune of the alphabet.

I tried again.

"You're blowing too hard. And puckering. You're not blowing out candles, Ruth. Watch me." She gave a long, clear whistle. "See? Let the air out gently, as you need it. Don't let it fill the space between your lips and your gums."

She did everything perfectly, and there was no hope of me being like her. Much as I wanted to, I couldn't make the sound. Elspeth's frustration increased, and we both felt better when I stopped trying. I began to sing instead, mixing two songs together: *ABCDEFG, how I wonder what you are.* Until then, Elspeth had never noticed that "Twinkle, Twinkle, Little Star" and the alphabet song shared a melody, but it was something I already knew. She watched me print all the letters of the alphabet along the top of my drawing in a crooked line, and she stayed quiet when I told her how the teacher always said we could be anything we wanted to be. "Even the girls," I added.

James tried not to concern himself with my future. In the evenings and on weekends, over a span of some years, he taught me about archery, beetle inspection, crazy eights, dominoes, ear wiggling, feather floating, goose chasing, haberdashery, ice fishing, joke telling, kazoo blowing, leapfrog, mimicry, nostril flaring, origami, papier-mâché, quick marching, reeling in, shaving, tie tying, ululating, vegetable growing, window washing, 'x's and 'o's, yodelling, and Zeppelins. I was an enthusiastic learner, not always quick, but not slow either. At school, my grades hovered right around average, which was nice, in a way, because average was something unusual for me. But there were things I excelled at, like patterns. Rectangle, square, triangle, square, rectangle. Once you understand them, patterns show themselves everywhere, solid and dependable. When I felt worried or afraid, I looked around for one and never had too long a search. They were on the floor and the ceiling, embedded in the rows of desks, stitched into jumpers and knee socks, locked in the whorls of my fingertips. There were the larger patterns too, when you saw things from a distance: the person in a house on a street of houses in a town of streets in a province of towns in a country of provinces in a continent of countries, and so on. Everything belonged.

Elspeth fretted about what went on at school, and felt sure that I got picked on, and James fretted about her fretting and said you could make something come true just by fixating on it enough. There was no proof that I was harassed, he said, and even Elspeth admitted it was just a feeling. She quizzed the teacher about my progress and my interaction with the other students, but the teacher waved her hand and disregarded Elspeth's concerns. "Children put each other in order," she said cryptically, without saying which of the children needed sorting. (There was a series of teachers like her, Miss Prue and Miss Gray and Mrs.

39

Ashcroft, just as there was a series of doctors with their own cryptic messages.)

Sometimes Elspeth wished she could hang with the coats at the back of my classroom, watching, her body falling in folds like the garments. And sometimes, from my place near the coats, I thought I could hear her breathing. How awful it would be if she knew that the things she imagined really happened: erasers twirling toward me and bouncing off my forehead and a bubble of laughter releasing all around me; the big laces of my shoes tied together by the boy who'd flapped my coat sleeves—I'll remember his name, Ronnie Griffiths, forever. Me rising when the bell rang, stepping forward, and falling to the floor. *Monster Girl. Horse Face.* Shame burned my eyes and ears. I looked up and saw Grace with her smudged glasses, pink in the face and grinning.

She can't help it, I told myself. *Everyone is laughing, and she wants to be one of them.* I laughed too as I pulled myself to standing. It was easier for all of us.

When I was seven and not yet too big for such an outing, James took me outside town, along a river that branched off ours, where we rented a canoe. It was a beautiful day. Birds soaring. The sky a blue dome patterned with scudding clouds. The quiet landscape carried on around us as though we belonged there. Our little factory town and the pulp and paper mill could be seen in the distance, chugging away.

James watched my back in the sunlight, my black braid that hung down and my spindly arms that worked the paddle. He liked being able to look at me without my knowing.

The sparkling water dripped from my paddle as it moved through the air. James closed his eyes. He heard a rhythm he wasn't aware of when his eyes were open. He could tell I was happy. Droplets sprinkled our faces as we zigzagged through the water and when James opened his eyes again he pointed out a great blue heron on the rocky shore. The giant bird turned and nodded, as if to acknowledge us. As James watched my profile grinning at the heron, he was overcome with a burst of optimism that these kinds of moments were sustenance for a child; there was a difference between living and existing. *We'll take a vacation,* he decided, recalling his own boyhood trip to the Maritimes, where he'd first seen the underside of a turtle. A wave of nostalgia and an internal slide show of memories: jagged rocks and seagulls, an island with cinnamon roads.

"Where would you like to go if you could go anywhere?"

"Um—the beach?" I asked, instead of answering.

In a flash he was there with thousands of soldiers, and he was pulling himself across the sand, over bodies, moving like a snake, and someone else's blood was running into his eyes—and then he was back with me again, forcing a laugh.

"It's not a test, Ruthie, it's a choice. If you could go anywhere in the world."

I let my paddle rest on my lap and thought about my private land with yellow roads. But it had to be a real place, a place I hadn't been. I pictured the globe in my room. "Egypt," I said, "for the pyramids."

James laughed again. "Pick somewhere a little closer, and I promise you we'll make it happen!"

As I spun the globe in my mind, James played out the argument he'd have with Elspeth, and wondered when she

41

had become someone who resisted rather than embraced. There was always a reason *not* to do something—but at some point she must have been different, because after all she had made it here. She would not want a vacation because there was no money, there was no time, and everywhere we went people would stare. This last reason would go unmentioned but it was the most relevant of the three. They stared at me in the grocery store and in the park and at the beach and on the trams and buses and in elevators and at the doctor's office and the dentist's and at the winter fair and in the cinema, and even at church, where we went only two times a year. God should forgive our habitual absence, Elspeth reasoned, for he knew what the rest of the congregation whispered. "That's the Brennan girl. She's only seven years old! It isn't any wonder they haven't had more children." As we drove home along the gash of a river, Elspeth would say to James, "You would think that in the House of God—" breaking off because my big ears were listening. As if I couldn't be hurt by a truth kept silent. I felt Elspeth's disgust for them. But none of it lessened her fervent, almost desperate belief in God, and none of it inspired me to seek him.

By the end of our paddle James and I were tired. As he pulled the canoe out of the water, his enthusiasm for our holiday fell away in pieces. He felt scorched by the sunshine and his shoulder hurt from paddling. My new sandals had rubbed my baby toe raw and I was whining.

"Dad," I said. "There's a blister!"

Every word that came out of my mouth was a high-pitched whinge. Walking back to the car, James held hands with me, though I was barely a head shorter than him now. As he drove us home he had to suppress the fear that had lately come whenever we got in the car, that if one day it would be too small for me, what then, what on earth then? Was such a thing really possible? He pushed the foreboding back down, reminding himself of what the doctor always said: *Nothing seems to be wrong.*

We moved through the landscape of leafy trees, on toward the town with its smokestacks and traffic lights. We rumbled across the bridge and with every bump little whimpers worked their way out of me. In the driveway James switched off the engine and just as he turned to me a whine came again.

Flushing red, he leaned into me and hollered, "BE QUIET!"

How a face can change in a moment.

Once inside the house, he released me to Elspeth. He loved me, but it was always good giving me over. He flopped onto their bed and slept through supper until evening, and I knew, though it had never been mentioned, that the possibility of our holiday had evaporated. When he woke he found he had drooled on the pillow, or maybe he'd cried. He thought of the afternoon, the canoe's slender bow splitting the water. The sound of the paddle and the creaking boat played in his head like music, like a melancholy song lodged there, and that bothered him more than his shoulder or his sunburned skin, for surely it had been among the happiest of days.

James and Elspeth's bedroom was rose-petal pink, a radiant shade. It seemed, stepping in, that not just the walls had been painted, but somehow the air was pink too. There was something calming about this room, where the curtains were always closed and the light from the bedside lamp was golden. The lamp sat on a doily made by my grandmother, a little scrap of cloth saved from a vanished life. For me she existed only in photographs. She was closed up in an album with my grandfather and Elspeth, who, amazingly, had once been a child. But not like me. Never like me. I loved to pore over pictures of Elspeth as the little girl Elsie, so pretty in her loose cotton dresses. The boy beside her in the photos is Stanley, her fair-haired little brother, who had a passion for cavies. I could see the cages stacked up behind him in the photo, stretches of wire framed with wood. One of the little animals sits on his shoulder, nuzzled into the crook of his neck, and I decided, looking at Stanley, that he must have been just like Dickon from *The Secret Garden,* who befriended wild creatures and knew how to make himself look like grass and trees and wood. I tried to picture myself in the Secret Garden with Dickon, surrounded by roses, but it was an inconceivable scene; I knew I didn't belong there.

Elspeth's bedside table held nothing but the doily and the lamp. A single dust mote sat on the dark, polished wood, like a star resting on tiny, pointed feet. On James's side, there was also a table and lamp. The clock was there too, and had to be wound regularly so he would wake up in time for work. He was a sound sleeper, and the room, so dark, so quiet other than the *tick-tock,* would hold on to him every morning if he let it. Often he wanted to. It was peaceful there upon the feather pillows.

There were no pictures on the walls, no knick-knacks on the dresser, which stood tall and plain against the wall, facing the bed. The first three drawers were for her and the bottom three for him. In with his socks and underwear was a velvet box that held an army ID tag and also a pair of cuff-links, never worn in my lifetime, but in their wedding portrait one winks out of his suit sleeve, against his crisp, white shirt.

The wedding picture, the room's only adornment, sat on the dresser and shows James in uniform, his arm wrapped around his bride's waist, where the taffeta is drawn tight and spills to the floor. At Elspeth's neck a glass pendant hangs from a fine chain. Her diamond earrings were given to her by James the night before this day: Corporal James Brennan, who found his bride in a hat shop while looking for a gift for his mother.

Looking at the portrait took me through to an earlier time when James and Elspeth were not my parents. The couple in the picture were like characters from a made-up tale, I could shape them and reshape them. They could be whoever I wanted them to be—the tiny dolls from my dollhouse or larger-than-life people like Anna Swan and Martin Bates, a giantess and a giant who fell in love and travelled together through Europe, befriending kings and queens. When they married, Anna's bridal gown and her towering hairstyle were festooned with orange blossoms. Martin wore a military uniform with fringed, shimmering *epaulettes*. But in my version, James's head pokes up out of Martin's stiff collar and Elspeth's rises from the ruffles of Anna's gown.

Elspeth is stepping down the church aisle towards James in huge, dainty shoes. There are bits of rubble in her way and she must step carefully to avoid them. Her little father is beside her, wearing his cardigan with its pockets full of rocks, and he has a terrible, shell-shocked expression as he

45

grips his daughter's arm. I am here too, an anachronism as well as an anomaly among the million tiny people filling the pews and stretching down the street in an endless line. Sunshine spills through the cracked church steeple; there are pigeons peering down from the fault line. Beyond them, a warplane crosses the strip of blue sky, its engine loud, then muted. Elspeth's old, rangy aunties look up, shielding their eyes as the plane passes, both giving the pilot two thumbs up. Elspeth's mother is here too, in the front row with Elspeth's brother Stanley and a row of heads from the hat shop. A guinea pig sits in Stanley's lap.

The day has been billed as the union of the Tallest Couple in the World, a sort of fairy tale wedding that will lead to a marriage bigger and better than an ordinary one, but the bride's veil is crooked and her shoes pinch, and the war still rages outside. It touches all of us, no matter how big we are, no matter how strong. From a distance the bride sees a gold button fall from her groom's giant uniform, spinning to the floor. She stoops to retrieve it, though the real Elspeth would never stoop with all those people watching—not for James or for anyone. It is too much to ask.

Looking on, I feel frustrated knowing what I know, but unable to change things. If only she understood the importance of such a gesture—placing the button in his hand and squeezing her own closed over it.

Alone in my room on the day of the canoe trip, I poked at my watery blister. I didn't yet know of Robert Wadlow, the young man who could touch the tops of traffic lights. In the year of his death, just as the war was beginning, he was twenty-two years old, stood eight feet, eleven inches tall, and weighed 491 pounds. And yet he had a wispy, fragile quality: a lanky body, spindly limbs, the hairless face of a boy. His feet were so far from his brain that he could barely sense them. His joints had warped under his own weight, and the leg brace he wore to help him walk chafed away at a blister on his ankle until the raw spot was infected. And he walked on, not knowing that the infection was moving through him. When the doctors tried to save him, it was too late.

My own blister would not kill me, and was less painful than James's harsh words. In the oasis of my yellow room, I crept back from the sting. From the ceiling hung fourteen model airplanes that twirled when I entered, and seemed to be greeting me, beckoning me.

Already I had to duck when I walked beneath them. I was getting large enough to wear Elspeth's clothes and shoes, and I would try them on, rushing so that I wouldn't be caught, seeing in the mirror how wrong I looked, how unlike her. But soon I was nine and, to my great relief, had outgrown anything worn by Elspeth. In the privacy of my room there was only me in the mirror to compare myself to. I would come home from school, walk down the hallway past the praying hands and the dressmaker's dummy, grasp the glass knob and turn: open, enter, close. Release of a long-held breath. I'd lie on my bed with my shoes on and look at the planes, listen to the balsa wood wings *tap-tap* against each other until they settled and were once again still. Balsa trees grow quickly, sprouting waxy flowers that open at night. The trees are short-lived, though. They grow in a hurry because they have only so much time.

47

But I look back with tunnel vision; I forget all of the normal days, in which Elspeth, James, and I sat together listening to the radio or playing cards, comfortable in our family routine. In the spring we planted flowers, and on summer evenings we sometimes set up the croquet hoops in our backyard. Mallets knocking against the painted wooden balls. In the fall we raked the leaves of our maple tree into a mountain, as any family would. At Thanksgiving and Easter and Christmas, the aunties Franny and Bea sent packages from England, full of sweets and fancy teaspoons and Marks & Spencer nightgowns. We dined with my grandparents on James's side, and Uncle Norm and Aunt Tess. It was always my job to set the table, and then afterwards to clear it, to wipe away the crumbs from the tablecloth with a little tool Elspeth had, a brush that lifted the crumbs and rolled them into a box that was also its handle. Uncle Norm, who had been a foot soldier like James, said that if it wasn't for the war, we wouldn't have such nifty modern conveniences, and though I didn't quite know what he meant, from then on I always thought of the war when I brushed the table clean.

The mundaneness of everyday life must have taken up most of our time, but in my memory it occupies the smallest sliver. So I say with honesty that this version of my life is just that: a version. It has been said that my condition may affect the memory, and anyway, it's not for me to decide the absolute truth of things, or why *the* truth might not be *my* truth. Even from my great distance, I am just too close to say.

The doctor measured my head and looked in my mouth, ears, eyes. He tapped my knees and my back and took my pulse and my blood pressure. His hairy fingers pressed on my stomach and my neck, and I could feel my heart racing with the chance that he would find whatever he was looking for—something wrong with me—but, as with every year, my body held on to its secret, and he pronounced me "healthy as a horse" and released me. I thought of the taunts, *Horse Face* and *Monster Girl*. I said nothing about my headaches or the shooting pains in my shins. The sense of my muscles stretching inside me, the tendons pulled thin. When he asked me, "How do you feel?" I said, "Fine. Thank you." Just the way I had been taught. He put a note in the file for Ruth Brennan: age ten, six-foot-two.

In the car on the way home, I felt the tension drinking up the air. James was clenching his teeth, and I could see the little muscle working in his jaw even as I tried to focus on the pattern of the street lamps standing at attention by the side of the road. Finally he said to Elspeth, "I'd like to think he's right. But we should get another opinion."

Before he could finish she was already hissing, "Ssshhh," and jerking her head back to me.

Like her I didn't want to discuss it, or even to hear it discussed. Nothing was wrong with me. Yet I stayed home from school as often as I could, professing bellyaches or sore throats—less worrisome than my real symptoms, one of which was loneliness. But then I would imagine myself growing bigger and bigger, confined in my little bedroom. The Cornish giant, Antony Payne, stayed so long in his room that when he died, his corpse would not fit through the door and could not go down the stairwell. To get him out, they

49

had to lower the floor to ground level. But who were *they?* Who sawed through the joists and the floorboards? At least if a soul dies with a body, then in death there can be no indignity. But in life there is plenty. In time I would find out everything I could about Antony Payne and so many others —like Anna Swan, the one who'd married Martin Bates. Before she met Martin she'd followed the path of other misfits and ended up at Phineas T. Barnum's American Museum, where curiosities showed themselves to the curious, the pity going both ways.

One muggy July day, a fire broke out at the museum, and Anna found herself trapped on the third floor, with the sound of screaming animals ringing in her ears. Bears, lions, kangaroos perished, though the human curiosities were quickly saved. But the giant girl couldn't fit through the burning doorways, and even if she could have, the weakened stairs might have snapped under her weight. Anna's best friend, the Living Skeleton, stood by her as long as he dared, but as the heat increased he could feel himself melting. And he was such a delicate creature already, needing to keep a nourishing flask of sweet milk on a chain around his neck. He lifted it toward his friend now, but Anna shook her head no. The perspiration rolled from her face as she watched the Living Skeleton leave her. Isaac was his name—important to remember that he had one. He had been a cobbler in another life, she recalled, as she listened to his shoes cross the floor. The flames popped and hissed. They poked through the floorboards and raced up the corners of the room. Then a window crashed, and Anna thought at first it was because of the intense heat, but faces appeared, and a derrick, and then the walls on either side of the window were bashed away too. Anna gathered her skirts and ran to the open space, crunching over the glass. She climbed out onto the derrick and they tied her to it, and when she looked below she saw that a crowd had formed, applauding her escape. Among the ordinary people were the Living Skeleton, the Fat Lady, and the Littlest Man. How small they looked as she hovered above them! Eighteen men held the line as they lowered her to the ground, and she could feel her face burning from the heat and from the humiliation of needing such special treatment. She couldn't lift her eyes to meet the gaze of the onlookers, and she was thankful that a carriage was waiting for her. She squeezed herself into it and heard the crowd mutter as one, amazed that a little princess coach could contain such a great lady. The carriage whisked her away from the burning building, and she sat hunched inside, holding her big knees, head pressed to the ceiling, skirt ballooning around her.

It certainly was something to feel my body elongating, opening out like the largest telescope that ever was. I kept outgrowing my surroundings—not just my shoes and underwear, but my chair and bed, the bathtub. All the places meant to hold me comfortably so that I could just let go and be myself. My toothbrush lost in the palm of my hand and fluttering against my teeth like eyelashes. The very walls of my home shrinking. In some ways it seemed that the external things were getting smaller while I was staying the same. The idea of my room contracting with me inside it gave me the feeling of suffocating, and when I thought about that for long

51

enough I'd find renewed enthusiasm for the outside world, whatever its complications. When I did go to school, I rushed as quickly as possible across the bridge, and took back alleys the rest of the way, staying out of sight as long as I could. The sparrows chirped and chattered in the trees as I approached, but stopped whenever I walked by, and stayed silent until I'd passed. Then they'd start up again, just as if they were talking about me. The mourning doves were kinder. They stayed at the edges of the alleys, their muted greys and browns lost among the leaves and wild grasses. I was like that great blue heron James and I had seen; I didn't belong among them. Yet I kept my class picture in my bedside drawer and studied it daily, naming each child and memorizing all the things I knew about them, drawing their likenesses with great care on foolscap paper and then labelling each sketch, only to tuck it away beneath the photo. The boy with the ring of dirt around his neck had been with me since kindergarten, as had Grace—her eyes were still crossed, doubled in size through her thick lenses, and I loved her more than the others though in all our years together we had hardly spoken. Ronnie Griffiths, sleeve flapper, shoelace tier, was long gone, but there was no end of replacements for his kind. Boys who stuck out a foot in the hall, sending me flying; girls rippling with laughter as they slipped their tiny feet into my shoes.

In the front row of school pictures, the most delicate girls sat with their hands folded and their ankles crossed, the way Elspeth did. Little ladies in picture-day dresses. Grace was right in the centre of them, and I was two rows behind, in the middle at the back. Tip of a triangle, or more like a solitary mountain. But look at my smile! If only I could drink something, eat something to alter my height, like Alice in

Wonderland, then there would be nothing to set me apart. But as it was I inched up, faster and faster. Curiouser and curiouser.

Could they see me growing? Could they hear the ringing in my ears? And was the ringing the reason that I didn't know the answers to the questions the teacher asked? What does a miller do? My panic rising. Make hats? Saw wood? Gather wind? Or was it just that I was so afraid I couldn't concentrate? I no longer trusted the answers that came to me when I sat in class, and I kept quiet, hoping that no questions would be asked of me. Could I do this my whole life? Could I sneak through?

For days I stayed home, avoiding delivery of my oral book report, but the assignment waited for me, and in a daze I found myself there in front of the class, wearing my lucky dress with seven pockets, reeking of shame. Sweat formed under my hair and trickled down my forehead. It slid down to my eyebrows and then dropped from that great height to the linoleum like a stream of shining pearls. I could hear muttering and giggling. The teacher hissing, *Sssshhhh,* making everything worse. Each pocket of my dress had something inside meant to bring me luck—a strand of blue yarn, a penny, a pink barrette that Grace had dropped and I had been too shy to return, an old fair ticket, a button, a paperclip, a bead—but one by one, I could feel each of them failing. Me losing my will to be upright, eyes closing, knees buckling, falling to the floor in a dead faint. When I came to, I kept my eyes shut as everyone whispered around me. Stroke of brilliance for a stupid girl. Now I would be allowed to go home.

53

As in my infancy, Elspeth pampered me. She brought me hot chocolate and cold apples cut into wedges. I loved her for not talking about what happened at school, but I very nearly asked her, time after time, "Will it always be this way? Will they always hate me?" Taking myself ahead to the moment where she didn't know what to say stopped me. After all, it was good to be home.

I moved from my bed to James and Elspeth's, to the couch, napping like a cat and awake in the long hours of the night, just as the balsa tree blooms. In the background, at any time of the day, I might have heard the sewing machine droning, or the *snip-snip* of scissors as Elspeth with a mouthful of pins added gussets and cuffs and panels to my already patchwork clothing. I knew how the pretty things in her closet disappeared and blended with my clothes to make them longer, bigger, wider, and even when I was very young I was aware of the care she put into altering my clothing. The perfectly finished edges, the secret pockets like gifts with satiny lining. Sometimes a hidden monogram, *RFBB,* as if any of my clothes could be confused with someone else's.

One afternoon, I was listening to her sew when I found a book in my parents' bedroom. I was lying on their bed and I slipped my hand under the pillow, trying to find a comfortable position. I peeked beneath to see what it was my hand had touched, and saw the grotesque image of an enormous man, and the red words that made up the title *The Giant Who Had No Heart in His Body.* The words formed an arc above the giant, who stooped over a girl riding a wolf. The giant had a mean face, wild hair, and a jutting, scruffy chin. A tooth was missing from his scowl. I slid the book back under the pillow and laid my head upon it, and as I rested, the story moved up through the cloth and feathers, showing me a princess riding a horse through her family's kingdom. She often went too far, but she always made it home again. Her horse was old and swaybacked, but it was trusty enough. Each time she rode, she ventured further, until one day she strayed outside the kingdom and happened upon a raven so starved he could not fly.

"Please help me," said the raven, "and I'll return the favour one day."

The princess chuckled to herself, thinking the pathetic thing could never be of use to her, but she had a bit of food in her satchel and so threw the raven some crumbs, since it was nothing to her. The raven devoured the food and flew off, and the princess and her horse galloped forward.

Further along she came to a brook where a bloated fish thrashed upon a rock. Its eyes implored her.

"Please help me. I need to get back in the water. I promise one day I'll return the favour."

The young woman smiled to herself again, thinking a fish could never be of much help to a princess. But it looked so pitiful as it choked and sputtered, and it was easy enough to poke it with the toe of her boot and push it back into the water. What was it to her? Nothing! So she did so, and the fish swam away gratefully.

Further along she came upon a wolf who lay dying. Its skeleton showed through its hide, and the smell of desperation rose around it.

"Please help me," the wolf said to the princess, dragging himself towards her on his belly.

"I'm sorry," she said, looking down at the wretched animal. "I don't know how I can help, as I have already given some of my food to a raven and nibbled the rest myself on my long journey. And now I am trying to get home."

"Give me your horse to eat," said the wolf, "and I'll be strong enough that you can ride on my back."

The horse was old and the wolf was so gaunt and desperate that the princess agreed. The wolf devoured the horse in moments, and afterwards was so strong that they rode off together in a flurry.

Just as the sun was setting, the wolf said, "The giant's house is just around the next bend. He is very cruel as he has no heart in his body."

The girl gasped with fear as the house came into view before her. A great shadow fell over her from behind, and, before she knew it, she had been plucked up by the giant's hand and taken captive.

The girl lived with the giant through all of the seasons, and would have been bereft were it not for the wolf who came to visit her each morning while the giant slept. One day he brought news that she would be instantly freed if she could find the giant's heart. So the girl grew wily. Each evening, after the giant returned from working his fields and unchained her, she fed him dinner: rack of lamb, roasted potatoes, and sweet pudding for dessert. He washed it all down with an ocean of wine that made him quiet and calm.

One night the girl asked the giant, "Where do you keep your heart?" and he laughed at her and said, "Why, of course, in a hole in that oak tree!" He pointed through the window.

But the next day when she told the wolf and he looked in that spot, it wasn't there. The same was true each subsequent time the giant told the girl where his heart was: his heart was not in the woodshed or under the porch step, as he had claimed. The wolf would return and look at the girl through the window, past the giant's sleeping body; he would slowly shake his head. And the girl would sigh. The more they looked for the giant's heart, the more elusive it became.

Yet the girl persisted. Then, one evening, after the giant had gobbled down his dinner and swallowed his wine, after the girl asked him, "Where do you keep your heart?" she added, "I'm so fond of you that I can't bear to think of you without it." The giant opened his mouth to laugh, as before, but no sound came out. Very solemnly he answered, "In a far-off lake there is an island, in which is a well, in which swims a duck, in which is an egg, in which is my heart."

She knew from the look in his eyes that it was true.

As the giant grumbled and snored through the night, the wolf tore through the countryside. When he reached the lake, he passed the message of the heart to the fish the girl had helped, and the fish swam across to the island, where he passed the message of the heart to the raven the girl had helped, and the raven flew to the edge of the well and called down to the duck, cawing and cawing until the duck fluttered up and off its nest, and there lay the egg, gleaming. The raven retrieved it, and took it to the fish, and the fish took it to the wolf, and the wolf took it to the girl, who kept it in the pocket of her apron all day until the giant came home and unchained her.

As they were sitting together at dinner, he with his rack of lamb and potatoes and tumbler of soothing wine, she pulled it from her pocket and held it up for him to see. He blinked and opened his mouth to say something, but just then she squeezed the egg in her palm, and the giant himself burst into a thousand pieces.

At the edge of adolescence, I soared past six-and-a-half feet and needed three naps to get through the day. My thirst was unquenchable. I guzzled water whenever no one was looking, because I feared what it meant, and if someone else knew it made the danger more real. What if the food and drink I ingested fed whatever was wrong? I hated my gluttony, and I knew how I looked from the outside, wolfing down my food. The belief that I grew because of my own greed—that it was my fault—became my most painful suspicion.

From the back I looked like an adult, tall and thin, but face-on my childishness still blazed out. My round eyes held a look of expectation and of not knowing what to expect, and it reminded Elspeth of when I'd been a toddler, eager to explore but ignorant of the risks. How stressful it had been for her to watch my every move. This was like that too, though I was past full-grown.

One bright, cloudless day I tripped off the back step and was unable to lift myself to standing. Again and again I pushed my palms into the grass and tried to heave myself upward, but my legs buckled beneath me every time, and my arms were useless. The sound of my voice made me shudder as I called for help, and Elspeth appeared at the back door, looking out at me. For a second she did nothing, and I was afraid I would have to say what I needed.

Can you help me please?

Can you get me up?

But then she moved toward me and put her hands under my armpits. It was so awkward, touching that way, breathing on each other. She was so much smaller. But I struggled up, then eyed the bits of dried grass on my clothes.

"Thank you," I said, without looking at her, and I brushed myself off and carried on, away from her. Her eyes went with me. I could sense her watching, feeling sorry for both of us.

We never spoke of the incident, but it stayed with us. It exacerbated her need to be near me, but on James's salary alone our financial situation had become precarious. I had already grown far past the bounds of normal, and there were so many things that needed to be custom-made with my steady growth—not just my clothing, which kept Elspeth up in the wee hours, but my shoes and boots. I slept diagonally, with my legs curled, but I needed a longer mattress, a chair that would hold me, and a table that I could pull up to in order to eat my meals "like an ordinary person," as Elspeth always said. I hated that phrase. But hated more that I knocked the table with my knees or elbows, spilled drinks, and shattered china. We couldn't afford for things to be broken.

Elspeth knew James was right when he said she needed to work.

"Ruthie already gets to and from school alone with no help from you—that is, when she goes," he added in a disapproving tone.

He didn't realize that in fact she followed me, dashing unseen from tree to tree through our neighbourhood, even soaring across the bridge behind me and praying I wouldn't turn around and see her. Then back behind the trees again as we continued to the west side of town. She noticed the way I walked with my head tilted to the right, and how I would emerge from the back lanes with a tentative manner. Sometimes she could see just the edge of my face, and the way it beamed if another child fell in step beside me, and she would rush along the hedgerow, muttering under her breath, *Walk with her, please walk with her. Walk the rest of the way with my girl.* Then her obsession would switch from worrying about me being alone to worrying about what the other kids said to me. She strained to listen, as if hearing the words allowed her to manipulate them. When I disappeared through the school doors some of her anxiety went with me, because there was nothing she could do now, it was out of her hands. She stood at the river's edge with those dark circles under her eyes, looking across to the factory where she had worked, and sensing how it buzzed with energy.

61

On the walk home, she promised herself she'd give up the ritual, but before she knew it she was snooping in my room for clues about how I was feeling, what I was thinking, what I might need that she could possibly offer. But the planes and books and dolls and stones and leaves and the endless sketches of herself and James and me—none of it revealed anything. As she left the room, guilt gnawed at her like a little virus blooming, but it didn't stop her from going back to my room later and looking around more. Picking things up, putting them down. A kind of compulsive devotion. She didn't know what she was looking for, but it bothered her that she didn't find it. She'd sit for long spells on the chair in my room with her hands in her lap, and it reminded her of her days at the hat shop window, before James appeared. What if he had never come? Would she still be sitting there?

It was this image of herself, pathetic and alone, that finally propelled her back to the suit factory after more than a decade away. As though she'd never left, she stitched pockets while the needle whirred up and down before her and a small, hot light illuminated her work. Pocket after pocket after pocket. How many suits had been made on the premises? She had no idea. Thousands, millions. The factory had existed decades before Elspeth's time, although during the war it had suspended regular operations in order to turn out uniforms for soldiers. Some of the very women she worked with had been at the factory back in those days, and had had husbands overseas. Some of the men had not returned; others, only partly. Had she herself been here instead of in England, she might have stitched the pockets of James's uniform. So strange to think. Every animate and inanimate thing had converged and come through the tunnel of war at once, and now, on the other side of it, the snarl was still sorting itself out.

The suits the factory made now were fine ones, better than she and James could afford. She watched her fingers running a piece through and thought of a man's hand resting inside the quality fabric, coins and keys jingling, a wedding ring strangling a bloated, affluent finger. And then a flash came, of the doctor's hand waving all worry away. The great bolts of fabric were so tempting. How refreshing it would be to make one whole dress for me out of one kind of fabric rather than tearing and restitching everything I had, or turning her own clothes and James's into something for me.

Her work was mundane, but Elspeth enjoyed it for that very reason. There was no doubting what was expected of her, and there was no question that she was competent enough to fulfill those tasks. The workday passed quickly, easily. Every morning she looked forward to the fact that she had somewhere to go, and that it was a place that had nothing to do with her. Or did it? The hardest part of the job was its social aspect, the way the women flocked together at breaks, revealing personal stories. They squeezed each other's shoulders or stroked a hand with no invitation whatsoever, and they said things like, *We're here for you,* when it was probably not true. It was only one of a million things people said for the sake of saying something. Like, *How are you, oh I'm fine, just fine thanks.* They brought cream puffs and strudels, sickly sweet food for sickly sweet company.

"Did you know," she said to the others one day, in a rare and blurted contribution, "did you know that herringbone is named for the dead fish? The pattern. It's just like the skeleton after the fish is gone." Her brother Stanley had loved

63

herring—pickled, smoked, raw. She held the fabric up to show them and then returned to her machine, the cool presence of Stanley at her shoulder and the smell of the fish there too. She closed her eyes to savour the thought of him tipping his head back, dropping the fish into his open mouth.

The women didn't know what to make of Elspeth, and she didn't help them figure it out. They knew she was my mother, and that either Elspeth or James had to be responsible for the fact that I was so overgrown. Why else would they not have had more children, they mused when Elspeth was out of earshot. Perhaps they used birth control. Some said that soon it would be as easy as swallowing a pill, but even now you could use an IUD made of plastic. You just tucked it inside and got on with things as usual. Or maybe they used the old method and just didn't—*you know*. Squealing with laughter. Hushing each other.

Elspeth knew they talked about her, and yet each day at ten o'clock she had tea or coffee with the other women, some of whom had been there since her initial employment before I was born, and a gaggle of new ones who'd started later. At noon there was lunch and more chatter, and at three o'clock, tea and coffee. The women took turns bringing buttery scones and cookies, which at first Elspeth declined. She sat too straight in her chair, enduring the breaks and the chitchat with her jaw clenched, and anxious to get back to her trusty machine, to brown tweed and green gabardine. But after a month or so, she inched her chair closer. The woman who pressed the collars was sobbing. She had a fat, pink face and the frizzy red hair of a clown, and on sight, Elspeth had disliked her. But today the presser sat hunched over, tears dropping onto the carrot cake that stayed untouched in her lap.

"It's over," she said. "It's completely over. He said he doesn't love me anymore." The presser looked up at the others with red eyes and a swollen nose. "So I'm sure he won't start loving me again. You can't once you've stopped. I mean, can you?"

There was an awkward silence. Elspeth nibbled her cake as the others fussed over their friend Iris, whose flowery name didn't suit her. *It must be awful,* Elspeth thought, *to stand over the hot steam all day and have it billowing up at you. That's why she's so puffy and red.* She tried to imagine James loving another woman, and how the discovery might affect her, but neither thought made her feel anything at all. Even the word *divorce,* which should have been shocking, didn't unnerve her when it flitted through her mind. Yet when she let her gaze travel back to Iris, a wave of sorrow came, and something else, something so piercing that she averted her eyes. A sip of tea, a bite of cake. She looked again. Iris's lashes had darkened and stuck together in little points. Her shoulders heaved and the other women's hands patted her back. Elspeth wouldn't like people touching her but Iris didn't seem to mind.

After that day, Elspeth began to use the names of the women she had first thought of as Button, Lapel, or Zipper. *Morning, Martha. Sally, this crumble is delicious, the sour berries just make it, don't they? Edna, how are you doing today?* She had to admit (at least to herself) that something had shifted. She had come to appreciate this sense of community, even if she'd let nothing essential of herself slip into the mix. She felt like a person again, a woman among women.

James noticed the change. He saw how his wife became less heavy-hearted when she left him in the morning,

65

resembling the Elspeth of old, who, if you tickled her deep in her right armpit, would explode with laughter, joy infiltrating the features of her face. But she was also a new, more mysterious Elspeth whose existence was separate from his. Watching her go, he found himself recalling how she had come toward him carrying flowers the day they got married, and had danced with her shoes off at the reception. He'd wondered just briefly if she'd married him to escape a life in shambles, because he knew she was too good for him, and he suspected others could see it too. But he had been more in love with her on that day than on any one before, and since then his love had kept growing, sometimes just a little, sometimes in vast amounts. Sometimes it came like a violent blow that knocked the breath from him.

He recognized his capacity for love in me. Little else of him showed itself in me, except for the black hair and the particular blue of my eyes, and my affinity for drawing. But there was a certain moony quality about me that had to have come from him, and that revealed itself further when a girl moved in next door.

That very first day she waved at me with a spanned hand and then made her way over. It seemed both momentous and so normal, watching her walk across the grass toward me. She was someone I knew already, or had always known. She wore her hair in sloppy buns on either side of her head, and her skin had a sandy, sun-swept quality, as if she spent all of her time outside. She had a little brother who looked so much like Stanley had as a boy that Elspeth, watching us from the window, had to look away: fair hair, and delicate, elfish features, right down to the pointy ears. Elspeth shivered before dismissing him and returning her study to the girl. A small, wiry creature, electric in a dangerous way. Her hands flitted with the energy of insects, and Elspeth saw the spell coming out from her fingertips and wrapping around me like a tangible thing. I stood smiling, delirious, oblivious. My head hung down, and Elspeth imagined me saying, as in days of old, "Hello. I'm Roof. What does *your* name?"

"I don't like that girl," she said to James. "She looks like trouble."

James laughed. "What does trouble look like? I thought it would be bigger, somehow, or hairy."

He held her arm and led her back to the sofa, where a steaming cup of tea awaited her. He always made her tea on weekend afternoons, just at the time she desired it, but the offering was spoiled by the fact that he never steeped the tea long enough, and the bubbles that formed on top reminded her of spent dishwater.

Outside, I dangled over the new girl, grinning a foolish grin. My face was bony now; the skin stretched over it gave me a deathly appearance, but I nearly forgot about myself when I looked at her. She had hair like honey and big green eyes.

The family's belongings were unloaded from a pickup truck by men with tattoos. Chairs drifted by in the background; a floor lamp sauntered past; from a cardboard box came the mewling of kittens. I stood with my hands thrust into the pockets of my homemade pants, and had a feeling of floating. My upper back bulged. My heart hummed. One shoulder stooped toward the girl as I willed myself smaller.

I was six-foot-eleven the day I met Suzy Malone, bursting through my most rapid growth period and all the physical changes that went with it. Sometimes I grew an inch in

67

a single week, and I had trouble adjusting to the constant changes in my size. My arm span was greater than my height, and the way I stood, slouching, made my arms dangle longer still. I had long ago outgrown ordinary doorways, and had to duck to enter the rooms of our house. To climb up stairs I turned sideways, because my feet were too big for the steps. My voice was getting deeper, and sounding further away, as if I were disappearing inside myself. I had tunnel vision, but an eye for detail. In fact, I suppose this has always been true of me: I can hardly pull my eyes from the infinitesimal details to take in the broader picture, so vast and vague that I don't know what to make of it.

The day I met Suzy I had a bruise on my forehead from bumping into a doorway, and she had a faint birthmark on her left cheek, like a berry stain. My eyes kept travelling to it, then over to her ear where an earring glittered, up to the top of her head, and down, finally, to her eyes, green with flecks of amber. Over, up, down, over, up, down. My heart was clunking, and the pulp and paper mill was stinking in the distance, and I was praying that she knew it wasn't me giving off that smell, but there was no way to be sure. She was chattering about her bicycle, and did I know the best trails, and what was the fastest route to the beach, and did I have a bicycle, and why on earth not, and how anyone could be without a bicycle she didn't know because riding was just the best thing, believe her, she had done it for ages. She had never had training wheels or a tricycle, ask her brother—she'd just always had a perfect sense of balance, watch, and she lifted her foot behind her and lowered her upper body until she'd made herself into a T. There was a pause as she posed there, suspended on one leg. The only sound was me breathing and shuffling a little beside her. And then she began to fall and reached for my hand, gripping my fingers and laughing, and after she'd steadied herself and stood up again and taken her hand from mine there remained a tingling where she'd touched me.

"You have to get a bike," she said.

I just laughed awkwardly, trying to think of something to say, nothing coming—but I was already promising in my mind to do so, both to keep up with her and to avoid letting her down. I had already decided that from this day forward those were the most important things.

That night in front of my mirror I replayed our conversation, watching my face move in reaction to her words, seeing what she saw, and wondering if it was not so bad, especially from this angle or that one. I pulled my curls straight and held on to them, and I looked smaller already. If I could only figure out how to keep my hair that way. If I could freeze myself, just like that, and still manage to be with her.

In their pink room, Elspeth said to James, "We have to do something about that girl."

"What girl?" he asked. He sat on the edge of the bed with his back to her and removed his slippers.

Elspeth rolled her eyes. She gave his back a light, quick smack. "Pay attention!"

He laughed. "Oh, *that* girl. Why?"

"It's not funny. She'll get her heart broken, you know."

He chuckled again. "Why on earth would you think that? A friend is just what she needs right now. Really it's about time." James slid under the sheets and began to wriggle toward Elspeth, and he was about to say, snickering, "Don't you think it's also about time for—" but her face close-up was red with rage, and there were tears starting.

"Oh boy," he said. "Here we go."

"How can you! Ruth is not just any girl!" Elspeth shouted, but the shout, of course, was a whisper, lest it drift out of the room and down the hall, toward the yellow room. "For heaven's sake, James, do you think you could muster some concern for your own daughter?"

James glared at her. Very slowly, he said, "Don't ever accuse me of not caring. Ruth *is* any girl. She has a heart. She has a life to live."

He threw off the covers and sat up, stepping back into his slippers. He pulled on his robe and left the room and did not return until morning, and in all their years, through all their quarrels, this was the first such separation.

But as he lay in the hammock under the stars, he felt proud of himself. He remembered a quiet night during the war when he had slept outside and felt aware, just briefly, of his place in the universe. He'd lain on his back and tears of contentment had dripped into his ears. He'd heard them pooling. And he had realized that an invisible string connected each star to a person, and that therefore he had nothing to fear. No one did. That night he felt a similar contentment. He believed his words to Elspeth had for once come out succinctly, just the way he had intended, and with a certain poignancy too. He hadn't anticipated that. He'd often stopped himself from responding to Elspeth's remarks because he couldn't find the right thing to say, and because life itself seemed a muddle, a riddle, which he could not lay bare. But outside, the sky above James was clear, and he was small but specific beneath a full moon. The hammock held him like a great, cupped hand.

Alone in the bed, Elspeth too could see the moon through the window. It was either almost full or it had been full yesterday, she didn't know which. She felt glad to have the bed to herself, and moved to the middle and spread her limbs. It occurred to her that it would make things better if she went to James and asked him to come back, that she wouldn't even need to apologize and he would come. It occurred to her that her ultimate goal should be to make things better, and that not moving from the bed meant she didn't want to. But why should she always be the one doing everything?

At work, some of the women insisted that husbands and children smothered the very person who kept them all going; the mother, they said, was the nervous system of the family. The redhead Iris said that women had finally had enough and were fighting back. Though actually, Elspeth thought at the time, it was Iris's husband who'd had enough and left her. Still, Elspeth felt smug and unappreciated all at once, and though she knew she would never do so, she saw herself relating the exchange she'd had with James, telling the other women how he'd thought he could fix it all with a bit of snuggling. The women would know what she meant by that, and they would scoff and *tut-tut* as they slurped their tea. She felt vindicated just imagining the scene. She stretched her limbs wider yet, revelling in her loneliness, at least for one night.

71

Suzy Malone was fourteen, a little older than me, and worlds wiser. After she arrived, the roof of our house came off, the sky beyond was revealed, and the home was revealed to the sky. Birds flew over and looked down inside the house and saw for the first time that it was much tinier than it appeared to be from the outside. They saw the thinness of the walls dividing the rooms from each other, and they could see inside the walls as well, the wires and the insulation, and they wondered at the complexity of the house's structure; was it for protection, like the uniform and cap James wore when he strode purposefully outside, or the big shoes that covered my aching feet?

Elspeth never said so, but the house with no roof reminded her that a ceiling could collapse and land on the floor—she had seen it happen—and so the open space was oppression for her, just as for me it was freedom. I moved trancelike through the house as the walls and doorways were enlarged to accommodate me. All the renovations were for my sake, though it was never mentioned. A layer of plaster dust covered everything, and I, too, grew dusty. The white powder clung to my black hair. It collected in the folds of my clothes, in my shoes, in the contours of my face, making me ghostlike, but I had never been more alive.

At the house next door, raccoons knocked over the garbage bins. Late at night, I could hear them calling and crying to each other that good things had been found. They made a home in the chimney, and their silhouettes scrabbled across the roof, the mother with six little ones behind. Beneath them, the human family carried on. The curtains in the living room window were attached with clothespins visible from the outside, and stayed closed all day, as if someone inside was sleeping and mustn't be woken at any cost. Elspeth disapproved of the clothespins, the garbage, and of course the raccoons, while James suggested that the Malones just needed time to settle in.

"Give the woman a chance," he said. "She's on her own, poor thing. Maybe I should offer—"

"Don't," said Elspeth. "You've got plenty to do right here." And so he didn't.

Weeks passed and nothing changed. If the Malones' garbage got put out, it usually happened on the wrong day, and had to be brought back in again, which sometimes took the better part of the week, meaning it would not be put out by the next collection day either. The bins were stuffed so full the lids wouldn't stay on, and the garbage gave off a stench more fetid than the pulp and paper smell, like something live rotting. The marigolds that had been planted that spring by the previous tenants died from neglect and yet still managed to look like stiff soldiers guarding the perimeter. The lawn turned pale as straw, except for the rounded border that got watered by our own spinning sprinkler.

I couldn't see into Suzy's house, and wouldn't have had the nerve to look had I been able to, but she spied on me with abandon. She looked into the living room when she walked by on the street in her dirty sandals, and she looked into the kitchen from along the back lane. One day she caught my eye, waved, and motioned for me to come outside. No one had ever been so familiar, so casual with me, and I rushed to put my shoes on and get out to her before she changed her mind and wandered away.

I took big steps toward her on the grass and then stood there, wondering what I should say.

"Hi," I said. A weird sort of laugh slipped out of me.

She could feel my jellyfish eyes caressing the top of her head and she peered up at me, smirking.

"What does the top of my head look like from up there?"

"Oh," I said. I looked at the part in her hair, swollen with a black fly bite; her hair itself had strands that were blonde, red, and golden. "It's nice." I wanted to say, *Everything on you is nice,* but just thinking it made the blood rush to my ears.

We were midway between our two houses, and Suzy said, "Come and sit in the sun with me. You're really pasty. You'd look good with a tan."

I followed her across the grass, thinking that maybe I *would* look good, that there were all sorts of things that I could do that I'd never even thought of doing before. Suzy pulled out two lawn chairs for us and plunked herself into one of them, and ever so carefully I lowered myself down and wedged my bottom into a chair. I tried not to put my full weight into the seat of it, so it was difficult sitting there with her, our faces raised to the sun and my muscles straining, but every moment felt worth it until the stitches in the chair began to give way. I could feel them popping and heard the fabric snapping beneath me.

"I have to get going," I said, and tried to pull myself up out of the chair, but I was stuck, looking like an absolute fool in front of someone perfect.

But Suzy just grinned. "Let me help you," she said, and she eased the chair's arms that dug into my sides away from my body, and put the chair back on the ground. We were closer than ever, then. She was right beside me, holding my wrist, and she looked up and said, "Wow—you really are tall. No matter how much I see you I just can't get over it. You seem bigger each time."

"Yeah," I said, shrugging. "I know it's strange."

I turned to go, but Suzy called to me, "Strange, yeah. But pretty amazing too. See you tomorrow?"

Yes.

Suzy's mother Margaret had taken a job at the suit factory, but Elspeth doubted she'd keep it long. She had a cigarette burning beside her at all times, and more than once she scorched the fabric she was working on. She didn't take part in the discussions during breaks, but sometimes released a phlegmy laugh at things the women said, things that were stupid to her for reasons she didn't care to share. She always arrived late in the mornings, and as she passed Elspeth's machine a bad smell floated behind her. Each time, Elspeth paused and watched Margaret's thick back, flashing dagger eyes at the stout, tough-looking woman who'd brought Suzy into the world.

It was with Margaret's arrival that pieces of fabric found their way into Elspeth's bag every few days at the factory. Bits of lining or piping, or sometimes large cuts of flawed but quality fabric that would have been discarded. The first time she saw the material in her bag, Elspeth looked around for a clue as to who had put it there. But the other women were all busy with their work; they paid no attention to her. Should she take it? Was it stealing? What if she got caught? Just this once, she decided. But days later there was more, and she took it again and again.

Through the long summer, while our mothers worked at the factory, Suzy and I lay in the meadow behind the houses, face to face. Suzy's feet, filthy from her lack of socks and shoes, came just to my knees. I was so enamoured with her that she even succeeded in having me take off my shoes, and I had not done that in public, away from the safety of home, since I was a young girl and less aware of my differences. She undid the long laces and pulled from the heel until one foot and then the other was released.

"Are these homemade shoes?" she asked, turning them over in her hands and inspecting them.

"Sort of," I said. "Store-made, but especially for me."

She pulled my socks off and my face went hot. One of my toenails was twisted and ingrown—a curled, grey nail instead of a smooth, pink one—but my feet were otherwise like regular feet, if large and red and throbbing. I wanted to know if she thought that my feet looked more normal with or without my shoes on, but out of politeness I couldn't ask. What if she said with? That I should always keep them covered? I didn't want to know. Anyway, it was better to look away from my feet and focus on hers, dirty but pretty, with high ballerina arches. She was going to be a dancer some day, she said, or a singer.

We walked in the grass together and left our shoes behind, which for Suzy was no big thing but for me was a liberation. I looked down at her, with the buttercups all around, and memorized the image so I could draw it later, and keep it. I tried to watch her from the corner of my eye so she wouldn't see me staring, but she was in constant motion and I couldn't keep track of her. She could easily disappear from my field of vision, and then I'd almost gasp out loud, fearing I'd lost her. So I gave up pretending not to notice her. The feeling whirring inside me was familiar, like hunger—a thing that couldn't be denied—so even when she laughed at me, I didn't really mind. I knew I looked ridiculous, that she could see me from a long way off, the blue sky beyond my black hair, a cloud forming a hat on my head.

"I'm sorry," she said. She chewed her cheeks but laughed harder.

I dipped down, and my face loomed before her.

"Why are you laughing?"

"I don't know," she said. "I just feel funny. Like I'm walking with an ape or an alien. Or an elephant who can talk."

For a moment my head pounded and my vision blurred. But then I grinned at her and made an animal sound.

Whatever it took, I would keep her.

James and a few hired hands renovated our house that summer. When the roof was laid back on, it was glass in places, and let in the light that the stippled ceiling had always kept out. James grew blisters on his hands and dark circles formed under his eyes, to match Elspeth's. But he whistled, too—he was happy taking care of me. He put glass doors on my room, which opened out to the backyard. For days after, a cardinal came and knocked on my new doors with her beak. She was a soft red, washed with grey, but her face had a frightening intensity. She knocked as though trying to tell me something, and once, she followed me from room to room, appearing at each window with the same *rat-a-tat-tat*. Pretty as she was, she scared me. Eventually, she flew straight for me with the glass between us, and fell dead to the ground without me ever hearing what she wanted to say. At the time it was something of a relief, because I didn't want a message that would change the way things were, and messages always do. If you open yourself to receive one and then don't act on it, the message stays inside you. No one ever rushes to tell you that all is okay, they rush to tell you how it should be, or to warn you of what's to come. And I was happy; I didn't want to be warned. I buried the bird in the garden, right outside the doors to my room, and Suzy herself helped me push the earth over its body.

"I almost died once," she confessed as we crouched there together. "When I was a baby. I'm allergic to bees, and one stung me."

I felt my panic close in. Bees were everywhere in summer. They could be anywhere, even indoors. The perpetual ringing in my ears shifted to a low buzz and I glanced around to be sure there were no bees nearby. I locked eyes with her to convey my concern.

"But how do you—how can you keep safe?"

Suzy shrugged and let herself smile a little for my sake. "I don't want to hole myself up." She lowered her eyes and added softly, "I'm not afraid of dying."

But I was terrified to lose her. Why did there have to be bees? I wanted to rip up all the flowers James had planted, the ones that drew the bees. The tallest ones lined the path that led up to my glass doors, a dazzle of hollyhocks and goldenrod. I made Suzy promise never to use that path in daylight again, when the bees were awake and buzzing.

"Yes," she laughed. "I promise. Now stop, Ruth! Don't worry about me!"

At night she took the path often, sneaking along it to climb into bed with me. I was ecstatic to have her there, but nervous too—not just to be caught, but to be with her in such a quiet, intimate space. I kept my eyes fixed on the skylight and watched bats flit across the moon.

"Don't look so frightened!" said Suzy, laughing.

"Ssshhh!"

But she laughed more. I covered her face with my hand in an attempt to silence her, and had a startling, thrilling sensation: I could smother her with my bare hand if I wanted to. I could break her nose and flatten it with nothing more than my palm. I pulled my hand away, shaking.

Mostly, these nights, we lay awake talking. Once, at deep blue midnight, we spotted a falling star through the skylight. I told her that dinosaurs had been wiped out by something that had fallen from the sky, that the whole world had had to start over again several times because of similar catastrophes. And looking up at the single plane that still hung from my ceiling—a Spitfire—I thought to myself that war

81

was like that: one world war and then another. I told Suzy that as a girl I'd pretended to be a sort of dinosaur—a leftover, millions of years old, with a special power for survival. I watched her as I spoke, and liked the way the light and shadow moved over her face, the way she listened, ungiddy, to every word.

And then I went quiet and waited for her to tell me things. Sometimes she offered a rush of trivial observations, such as how Patrick smelled like tomato soup; other times she confessed that she missed her father, who'd been a medical orderly during the war. Her mother said that was just about the worst job a man with a weak stomach could do, and that it had ruined him. Suzy still had his dog tags, and a handsome picture of him in uniform taken before he had been ruined, but he had left the family long ago. Suzy's mother was beside him in the photo, planting a kiss on his cheek, and I was astounded by how much Suzy looked like the Margaret in the picture, and not the Margaret in real life. That a person could change so much. I thought, *But Suzy will never become what her mother is.*

"I'm never getting married," Suzy said, looking sad and serious.

"No," I promised. "Me neither."

Suzy smiled then, just a little. "Joke, right? Because who would ask you?!"

We laughed together until Suzy fell serious again. She said her father had knocked out her mother's tooth and her mother could dislodge the fake tooth and send it in and out on the tip of her tongue for a lark. The sight gave Suzy a terrible feeling and made Patrick leave the room.

"I miss my father," Suzy said, and after a pause, "but I

miss my cat more." She said the cat was white with two black rings, one around her eye and one around her tail. "Just before we moved, our cat was released into the wilderness with its kittens. The litter always reeked and the food bowl got all mouldy, so my mom said she'd had it. She really hates a mess."

I thought of the garbage and the clothespins, but I also thought, *Released into the wilderness* sounds nice, almost like a good thing to do.

"I've never told anyone about her tooth," Suzy whispered.

She snuggled into me and I breathed the smell of her hair. I felt in my own body how telling the stories left her dizzy and ungrounded. As she inched home through the flowers and the garbage with her heart rubbed raw, a raccoon looked in on me from the skylight, checking that I was okay, and then it clambered away on its sharp claws.

Though Suzy was sad, my heart was bursting—she was my ally, my only friend, and we would always be together, like aunties Franny and Bea. In a way I was glad for her unhappiness because it meant she needed me. She had *confided* in me. No one had ever done that before. I wanted to tell her that I'd never had a friend like her. Only Grace, to whom I had barely spoken. But Grace could not compare. What I'd felt for Grace seemed small and silly now. She was a cross-eyed figment of my imagination. Suzy was bright and alive, something I'd been waiting for since the beginning of time, and also nothing I'd ever expected. She was the collision of those two things.

One night she instructed, "Talk," and placed her finger on my throat.

I swallowed.

"Say something, Ruth!"

"I don't know what to say."

"I can feel your voice buzzing through there when you talk. It's a funny kind of voice, like it's coming through a tunnel." She rested the palm of her hand on my throat. "Ruth, talk!"

"What should I say?"

"Say anything."

"I like the shape of your head. How round it is at the back, like Nefertiti's."

"Ruth, it's just a head."

"It's nice. It's a nice head," I told her. And then closer, with my nighttime radio voice, just what I'd been wanting to say: "Everything on you is nice."

"Yuck, don't," she said. "It makes me feel sick when you talk like that." She lifted her palm from my throat, then pressed on it again.

"Your head's like a giant peanut," she said.

She tipped her head back and her mouth opened wide with a burst of laughter, and I said "Ssshhh!" as always.

"I'm sorry," she said, still laughing. "But it is! Your head is like a peanut!" She could hardly get the words out. "I never noticed before, but it's all long and kind of dips in and out again, like peanuts in a shell. God, Ruth, you make me laugh so hard I'm crying!"

Whatever made her happy was enough for me. I began to keep a cloth over my mirror, so as not to spoil my exhilaration. When I wasn't looking at myself, my love for Suzy covered up my self-loathing. By some miracle, it was bigger than me.

And it seemed so long since I'd believed in miracles, but I still remembered the thrill that anything was possible —mushrooms would grow behind my ears if I didn't wash well enough. If I swallowed my gum, my insides would stick together. The tooth left under my pillow when I was six had been whisked away by a fairy who'd put a shining coin there in its place, something I could spend on anything I liked. Then, one night, I'd woken up and seen James there, with a tooth in one hand and a coin in the other. We looked at each other, saying nothing. His expression had been hard to see in the dark, the response inside of me equally obscured. Was I guilty of something or had I been betrayed? I closed my eyes to let him make the exchange. When he left the room, I heard him whisper with Elspeth in the hallway. The rest of my teeth had fallen out without ceremony. Little by little I realized I had misunderstood many things, but more mysteriously still, the knowing didn't make me wiser.

With painstaking attention, James refurbished a bicycle to fit me, and just as he'd done when I was little, ran along beside me with his hand on the seat until he felt sure I was steady enough to ride on my own. Elspeth stood on the porch step, chewing the skin around her fingernails, eyebrows working. I didn't notice either of them; it was Suzy who kept me upright, cycling forward. And it was Suzy who wound a yellow string around my handlebars for good luck. "So you won't fall," she said. Inside, I promised to keep it

85

there always, and to follow her wherever she wanted to go. As long as she was ahead of me, singing all those songs she knew from the radio, I would follow. What a feeling of freedom it was! And what a sight we were, little Suzy and big me tearing along the horizon, and sometimes her brother Patrick, too, trailing behind us. An afterthought, a shadow.

Outside of town we stopped at a place where the train tracks crossed a narrow river. We dropped our bikes and sat on the rocks beneath the railway bridge with the water moving quickly past. It was white water, and loud, and we had to shout to hear each other. Suzy kept yelling at Patrick to go for a swim but he wouldn't.

"Okay," she said. "But if you want to stay with us you have to hang underneath the bridge when the train passes. Until it's gone right over."

"But Suzy—" I said. My voice disappeared beneath the roar of the water.

"Okay," said Patrick. "I'll do it."

"You have to climb up now and wait till it comes. Then grab on and hang."

"Okay."

"The whole time or you have to go home."

"I know."

I watched Patrick step over the rocks in his old sneakers and make his way up under the bridge. He climbed like a monkey and perched himself on a metal rung.

"Suzy, it seems kind of—"

"He doesn't mind. He likes it."

We sat watching the water and Suzy smoked one of her mother's menthol cigarettes. The smoke swirled above us and drifted off, and I looked up to see if Patrick was all right, but he looked just the same as before. Suzy dropped her cigarette in the water and it moved away so fast my eyes couldn't follow it. Then we heard the train in the distance, barely audible above the rushing water.

"Grab on!" called Suzy.

Patrick reached for a strut and swung himself out just as the train shot overhead. The water was so loud and the train was louder and Patrick was hanging there with his legs dangling. I could see his mouth moving but I couldn't hear what he was saying. His knees were grass-stained and his T-shirt rose high and showed his skinny middle. I saw his hands gripping the metal, and his body vibrating. I thought I could feel the train's vibration too, but it was just me shaking, quivering with fear. The horn blasted, and Suzy whooped with laughter and even Patrick grinned as he made his way back to the rocks. They had done this before, I realized, and my shaking subsided. It was nothing bad if they both understood it. Inviting me along must have been a form of welcome.

When we arrived home that day my parents looked smaller, and the modified house around them seemed all wrong. I could feel how our paths were diverging. Not just mine with theirs, but theirs with each other's. Increasingly Elspeth and James followed their individual desires rather than those that could be pursued together. James squeezed an array of new hobbies in between his household duties: squash and lawn bowling, beginner's Spanish, and advanced woodworking, which he could justify because of my constant need for renovated surroundings. He began to notice things he had always taken for granted, such as trees, and to puzzle through what made their roots grow in a different season than their leaves. While he was not a devout man, he thought he glimpsed the mechanics of some master plan that was beyond his knowing. But at Elspeth's whispered prayers, his eyes rolled.

"Who are you talking to?" he scoffed. "Maybe you should speak up. He's obviously hard of hearing."

Every Thursday, just as before, James sat on a bench by the river and ate a pressed ham sandwich. He liked to come to the river to acknowledge a watery day in his past without ever having to say anything about it out loud. As he looked at the ripples of water repeating, he realized that all the days of his future stretched out before him in an expanse of sameness he had neither chosen nor rejected. Thursdays, he ate pressed ham. The soft bread turned gummy as he chewed, and stuck to the roof of his mouth. Tomorrow would be Friday and a week would go by and then it would be Thursday again. He looked at the round face of his watch, at the second hand moving through the minute, which moved through the hour, which moved through the day and so on, right back to the beginning. He held his sandwich to take another bite and recalled the time I had bitten into a hot dog and come upon a pig's eyelid, with the lashes still attached. Being the man of the house, he had examined it closely, and he had never forgotten the way the lashes left an impression in the meat, like a fossil. Now, looking down at his sandwich, he said to himself, "I'm leaving," and without any action on his part the cycle had been broken. He had always wondered what prompted people to turn their lives upside down, for he was a man who valued constancy, but today he understood that the smallest, least relevant thing could be a provocation. Or perhaps the idea had begun long ago, in his subconscious, rattling and chafing there, waiting to burst through.

While he made the rest of his deliveries, his determination stayed with him. He felt giddy, as though he'd guzzled champagne, and then anxious, as though he'd followed it up with pots of coffee, yet he'd had nothing but one bite of his sandwich by the time his shift was done. Still, today he didn't hurry home. He returned to his spot by the river and watched the sun travelling in the sky, and marvelled at the fact that it was actually he himself who was travelling, though he was sitting still. Then he crossed the bridge and roamed the parts of town that were not on his mail route. How rare it was for him to visit these streets, with their duplexes and brownstones. This was close to home, but he felt he'd entered another world, as in his soldier days when he'd trekked over hill and dale with his equipment strapped on. Before he'd engaged in battle, it had seemed like an opportunity, the trip of a lifetime, yet one that he'd been paid to take.

In an apartment's windows he saw lights flickering on and then a person illuminated—a little man passing from one room to another. James imagined he himself might live in an apartment like this once his marriage broke up. Once *he* broke it. Shocking to think. But divorce was spreading, like a sickness or a fashion. It was often written about in the magazines he delivered to people's homes, which he sometimes scanned on his coffee break. So it was no longer just for celebrities. A thrill crept up his spine, and his stomach burbled, and he stood grinning at the window until the man returned and closed his blind. But James kept smiling.

Before he knew it he had crossed back on the second bridge and arrived in the bustling downtown, where people

89

scurried this way and that. Fat summer raindrops were falling from a single cloud, and when a gust of wind came and the sunshine returned, he stood beaming on the sidewalk. The smell of bread wafted from the bakery. Nearby, the florist's broom was making a *ch-ch* sound, and he admired the way the petal-garbage danced like bright confetti as she swept it into a pile. He thought about approaching her and announcing, *I'm leaving my wife,* just to tell someone, but he flushed, noticing the sway of her flowery dress and the bulge of her calves, and realizing how such a statement could be misconstrued.

Only when he made it to his own street did some form of sadness come over him and hold his feet to the sidewalk. The sensation of hands around his ankles was so real, so like a day he tried to forget, that it seemed they had pushed up out of the earth to grab at him. But when he looked down, he saw only his postman shoes, the laces holding fast. He continued toward the house, looking into the living room, where I lay drawing on the floor and Elspeth passed back and forth with the vacuum. He watched me chew the end of my pencil and he knew before she did it that Elspeth would nudge my foot with hers and I would raise my big legs so she could vacuum beneath them. Our actions looked like movements in a dance, the choreography all mapped out and the players stepping through in time with each other. For a moment it moved him.

And then his eye found the steaming bucket and mop at the edge of the carpet, and he knew that when Elspeth was finished vacuuming she would tackle the bare floors. She could never do just one thing in an evening. She even did the tasks she'd asked James to do before he got a chance to start them—or she would redo what he had done because it had not been to her standards—and he wondered if there wasn't some hostility behind that irritating habit, which always made him feel like a disappointing child. He knew that during dinner she would be eating, flexing her troublesome ankles, making the grocery list, finishing a crossword puzzle, and asking about his day without looking up from her paper.

Later James would say to Elspeth, *I'm leaving you.* Or whatever it was one said. He couldn't envision what would take place in the wake of that statement—or rather, he could only envision the things that took place every Thursday night. Even with a statement that changed everything, he couldn't picture anything changing. They would wash up together in the kitchen while listening to the news on the radio, delivered by the same snooty, articulate voice year after year. The heavy stories first, about murder on the large and small scales, and then the lighter ones, about dogs and children. They would comment on things. Then if there was no project underway in his workroom—furniture that needed resizing or a patch for a strained bicycle tire—he would retire to the room he could see now from the street, and as he looked in at the empty chair that had held him for so long in a loose, comfortable embrace, it was as if he was seeing into the near future, when he had gone elsewhere, and he had a great sadness for a day that had not yet come.

That Thursday, we ate in the dining room as usual. My large chair was on the floor, pulled up to the table that sat on a platform of pine boards along with James and Elspeth's chairs. James had sanded and varnished the platform, giving it an oak finish to make the odd structure fit in with the dining room set that had been a wedding gift from his parents. There was always something that needed doing, and most of it was for me.

As James ate dinner kitty-corner to me and across from Elspeth, he examined the cutlery in his hands, and asked, "Where did we get these? I mean, who gave them to us?" He ran his fingers along the pieces as though they were precious artifacts dug up from the ruins of an ancient civilization. Objects that might tell him something about the bewildering people who had originally used them.

Elspeth answered, but he didn't hear her. He was looking at her bare earlobe, and noticing the absence of a diamond there caused him to drift into a vignette of their wedding day, the day after he had given her a pair of earrings, winking up from a blue velvet box. For the ceremony, she had appeared at the chapel door, and he, heart ballooning, had watched her approach on the arm of no one, small and pristine. Such a contrast to later, when she'd wept in their room and looked at him with a desperate face and said (only this once) that nearly everyone she had ever loved she had also lost, and that was why she was terrified, she would always be terrified, she was sorry.

"Ssshhh," he had said. "You won't lose me. I can promise you that."

He had taken her shoes off, and rubbed her pinched, bony feet, and she had fallen asleep in her wedding dress and diamonds with crescents of black mascara under her eyes.

"Why are you looking at me like that?" she asked him now, voice spiced with animosity.

He checked himself and glanced at me, but I shrugged. I was inhaling my potatoes, thinking ahead to a second helping before the first one was done.

"Like what?" he said.

She made a mopey, puppy-love face, and his nostalgia withered.

Because I'm leaving you, he thought with a thrill.

And that night as she slept beside him, he looked at her eyes moving under her eyelids. He remembered thinking about her eyes before they were married, about how they were rich as topaz, and working up the nerve to deliver that little piece of poetry that now made him wince for his former self. The man who would say such a thing seemed like a different man, and the woman who'd heard it someone other than Elspeth. (Elsie, they had called her. Why hadn't he?) As though he were watching a corny movie, he saw himself and Elspeth standing in the hat shop with their fingers entwined. He was saying the words *rich as topaz,* and she was lifting her face to his, flashing her two jewels at him and locking him in place, and yet seeming also demure and refined. He smiled. He thought of waking her up and telling her what he'd been thinking about, because it suddenly seemed more funny than awful, the silly intricacies of courting and the bloated language of romance. But to do so would also be to say, *I've been lying awake thinking about us. Thinking way back to the beginning.* And she would know. She would have to know.

You are the love of my life, he said without speaking, and her sleeping face softened as he thought the words.

No. Of course he could never leave her.

On a hot morning in August, the phone rang just before breakfast. Elspeth was buttering toast and James was laying the table, so it was me who answered and heard the prim English accent on the other end of the line.

"Hello?"

"Hello. Mrs. Elspeth Brennan, please."

I watched Elspeth's hand rise and cover her crumpling face as she learned that the aunties had died—both Franny and Bea, together. They were out for a country drive, but something went wrong. A passerby noticed skid marks on the pavement leading to a trail of broken shrubs. He pulled over, got out of his car, and followed the path to a lake where the aunts' car had bubbled under. They were found inside, Franny in the driver's seat as usual, and Bea, having climbed across from the passenger's side, with her arms around her sister. No one knew what made the car leave the road, but Bea's window was open. If she'd wanted to escape, she could have.

Elspeth sank to the floor and cried with the phone buzzing in her hand, and James hurried toward her, crouching down beside her and smoothing her hair. I had never seen her sit on the floor before. The toast and tea grew cold in honour of Franny and Bea, of Gog and Magog. The real ones were just ordinary old ladies; the legendary versions descended from a Roman emperor. He had thirty-three daughters, every one of them wicked and wild, and he married them off to thirty-three men with the hope of taming them, but the daughters would not be subdued. One night, they slit their sleeping husbands' throats, a crazed act, or one of solidarity. As punishment, the daughters were banished from the kingdom and set adrift in a boat with their hair tangling in the sea breeze, waves churning beneath them. They came to an island inhabited with demons, and they mated with them, producing a race of giants. Gog and Magog were two of these, and grew to be the guardians of the city of London, chained to the palace gates.

I loved the aunties from afar, since their great stature put my own in context. And yet before Elspeth left for England, she showed me a photograph of herself as a girl about my age, standing between two women of regular size.

"That's Bea," she said, pointing, "and this one's Franny."

She seemed to have forgotten her lie that the aunts had stretched to six-foot-four, *at least,* and that, no, sorry, there were no photographs. Baffled to the point of speechlessness, I stared at the two women. Bea had a kind face and curly hair; Franny was slimmer and squinted into the camera as though she was trying to see me. Between them, Elsie had been caught with her eyes shut. But she grinned, so this was before the war, when the scope of the coming tragedy was unimaginable. In the photo, with its rippled white edges and varying shades of grey, she wouldn't look at me, so it was hard to tell whether or not to feel deceived.

I curled myself into the car and sat with my chin on my knees as we drove Elspeth to the airport. She could take the train, she said, but James insisted on seeing her off, which meant a long drive to the city and a kink in my neck that would last for days.

James carried Elspeth's suitcase as we walked through the airport. Heads turned to see the mother, the father, the gigantic child. I had never been in an airport before, and found myself itching to travel, as in my childhood when James would ask me to spin the globe in my bedroom and then tell me a story about the place where my finger had landed. It was because of this game that I had quickly learned the names of countries, and where they sat in relation to each other. I knew where he had been as a young soldier, but not what had happened to him in those places. And I knew where she had been when he'd found her, in a town in England, to which she was now returning. Three weeks she would stay, maybe four. My buttons would pop. My sleeves would creep short in her absence. I had never been separated from her before, but I kept my nervousness as secret as my excitement.

We said goodbye to Elspeth as if she were going downtown for groceries, and no one acknowledged that this was anything more than that, except we stayed and watched the plane lift off, and I looked through my trusty thumb-and-finger telescope until I could see Elspeth in one of the little windows. The plane carried her up and away, which was an amazing thing to watch from either vantage point. I could see myself get smaller in her eyes.

This was the first time Elspeth had ever flown. During takeoff, she felt a tremendous relief and a new, unnameable burden. She would be "home" in a matter of hours, though it had taken days to come to Canada by ship, and she and the other passengers—brides all—had endured seasickness and winds strong enough to blow a body overboard. Maybe someone *had* been blown overboard, she couldn't quite remember whether that had happened on her own ship or another. And now here she was, roaring through the sky at a phenomenal speed, but sitting with her hands in her lap, gazing out the window. She passed over the mouths of rivers, the foothills, and the heartlands. She saw from above the lakes that were formed when a giant's footprints filled with rain, the mountain ranges that are great bodies sleeping. As she crossed the belly of the ocean she counted the years since she'd been back: thirteen.

It was difficult to imagine herself as a young bride looking for her husband on the blank horizon. She remembered the clothes she'd worn that day—a pleated skirt and blouse she'd made herself—and she could see them now as if they were on her body, but she couldn't see herself, at least not the parts that counted, the face and the eyes. What had she been thinking then? Why had she agreed to come? When she thought back to them, the women on the ship—a thousand brides—they seemed just like the women of the factory, a group to which she didn't really belong. Why was that, when they had so much in common? They had all married Canadian soldiers. They had sat in bomb shelters with gas masks over their mouths. They had picked through rubble for lost things. Probably they had each lost someone, somewhere, over six years of war. They had watched the war dramatized on movie screens even while it continued around them, and they had noticed that the uniforms fit perfectly on actors but rarely so on real people. Maybe it was even true that every one of them felt as separate from the group as Elspeth did—perhaps they had that in common too. But the link was meaningless if no one spoke it into existence. The *Aquitania* that had brought her to Canada was a luxury ship with grand, decorous rooms, a favourite of celebrities in the 1920s but pressed into service as a troop carrier during the war, and the war had beaten it down. The *Aquitania* still had her wartime colours in 1946, the year Elspeth crossed—drab grey, the colour of rubble. To Elspeth, everything was grey then, and for a time after, and if it wasn't, it seemed garish or disrespectful. Or blatantly, selfishly naïve. So she crossed under a grey sky, on top of grey water, toward a grey horizon. And didn't it just say everything when James was there waiting for her in the crowd with a bright bouquet of flowers, a red rose in his lapel, a green tie, and a purple band around his hat?

But wait—there is so much to say before that.

In the summer of 1944 I share a bird's-eye view with rockets and warplanes as smoke from bombs disperses the puffy clouds that would otherwise linger in the sky over England. Elsie is twenty-one years old, and lives with her parents near London. She makes hats, but no one is buying them now, and the little hat shop that has been in the family for generations has instead become a gathering place where local women knit socks for soldiers. The heads that model the hats are bare skulls, lined up on the shelves at the back of the store; the hats are packed away in cedar boxes to be preserved for happier days. It is a time of waiting, of not knowing how long the waiting will take, or what it will bring when it's over.

It is also strawberry season, first the plain white flowers and then the fruit. The berries push out from the circles of leaves without any awareness of the state of the world. They expect it to be warm and sunny, and it is. Elsie fills pails with strawberries. The fruit reminds her of when she and her brother Stanley were little, and they would eat as their mother picked under the hot sun. Stanley is a soldier now. Just 19, he's been to all sorts of places he would never have otherwise visited. When at last he came home on leave, there was something sophisticated about him, something alien. He joked but she could smell his fear. Or was it hers? The freckles on his nose had disappeared, as if they were spots that could be brushed off at will, and at first she couldn't figure out what was different about him, what was wrong.

The last time she saw him was February. He had cut himself shaving and the nick glistened as he leaned in to kiss her goodbye. Their mother cried and blew her nose in her hankie, a loud, honking blow that made Elsie and Stanley exchange a familiar, stifled laugh. Their father, having stumbled through the Great War, saluted, and with his cardigan hanging down around him he seemed tiny and old. Inside his tattered slippers were feet that had once turned red and blue from trench foot, and had remained, years later, susceptible to the cold. He wiggled his toes as he hugged his boy, and reminded him to change his socks often.

And then Stanley was gone, by truck, by train, by ship, writing mystifying letters home that were fewer and further between, harder and harder to decode—if in fact they needed decoding. Was he trying to tell her something, or was he just writing about his days?

Dearest Elsie,

Can you believe two among us have been stung by what is called a "man of war," of all things? It's a kind of jellyfish with a long, dangerous stinger. The boys are paralyzed, moaning in the infirmary, but I am fine except for a fantastic sunburn, blisters and all. No more swimming for me. The men of war are as plentiful as U-boats in these parts, and a fearsome enemy. I want to go swimming, but don't worry, I won't. Please don't tell Mother about the jellies. I know how she worries.

Yours,
Stan

February, and now June. She picks only the ripest berries, the ones that drop into your palm as soon as you touch them. She picks two, eats one, picks two, eats one. The sun makes a blanket on her back, on her hair, so it's as if she's under the covers, like the cat, Louie, who sleeps purring at her feet. Louie is Stanley's cat, and he never liked her until Stanley was no longer around. The cavies, too, are kinder now that she is the one to feed them. But it's him they love, as all animals do. Once when he was a boy he came home from school trailing three dogs who wanted to be with him.

A bee buzzes, and then another. She hears her mother's voice from long ago, *Stay perfectly still and they won't bother you.* But the noise builds to a fevered hum. The seconds pass so slowly, giving her every opportunity. There is the sound of sirens, the cue to run, but Elsie sits still. A shadow passes, turns her legs grey as they stretch before her. Somewhere nearby, the bombs scream down, the ground shudders. Elsie sits in the meadow with her eyes closed, the pail of berries on her lap. These latest bombs are actually rockets with no pilot to sacrifice—doodlebugs, they call them, a name so ridiculous she can't bring herself to say it. The bees hover over the strawberries, and she can feel the whir of their wings against her fingers. She waits. When everything is quiet she opens her eyes.

Something has happened, she knows that, but a dead calm protects her as she walks home along a street cluttered with bricks. The church has cracked open. Houses have tumbled in on themselves and spilled out over the pavement so that everyone's personal things are on view. An invasion. There are chairs and pots, books and clothing, a piano, and a teacup sitting unbroken in its saucer. Other things have exploded beyond recognition. Somewhere under it all is her father in his cardigan, her mother. But the hat shop with the house above it is still standing. Not even the glass has cracked, and the heads lined up at the back of the store stare out.

For Elsie, this is the only slowed-down day in all of the war—longer even than that Blitz night in May, years ago now, when London flamed and she watched it burning from a distance, sitting high in a tree with Stanley. This day goes on and on, into the night, lit by balls of blue and orange blazing and turning in the sky like planets rushing too close. At the end of the road, the aunties appear, Franny and Bea, with their sturdy shoes and their handbags, the kind that hold everything, despite being compact with tidy snap closures. Into the handbags go Louie the cat, his food bowls, Elsie's toothbrush and nightgown, a bundle of Stanley's queer letters, and a book of photographs that can't replace the lasting image: Elsie's parents under the bricks. She opens the doors to the cavies' cages and releases them, and before any of it has begun to seem real, she is on board a train, with the aunts at her side like crutches, and they are off to somewhere safer.

The aunts have procured a farm in the country until the city is livable again. Elsie doesn't ask for details, and is

103

thankful to be in an anonymous space, where it's easy to slip into another existence. The aunties function as man and wife, meaning the unspoken things are the greatest barrier between them. They bicker the way married couples do, and one evening over throat-burning whiskey Franny suggests that the world *needs* war; that men do. They need the release that comes from fighting, defending, maiming, saving, killing each other. The chance to be heroic. "Then we should get rid of men," says Bea, and they cackle and pour more whiskey. Bea does the cooking and cleaning, and Franny trims the hedges and puts out the garbage and sets the mousetraps that are of dire necessity in such a drafty, old house. Mice move so quickly, so silently, they make you wonder if you are seeing things. They can disappear into holes no bigger than a coin, so they come in and out as they please, skittish with fear, but persistent. Bent on surviving. Elsie dreams of them scampering over her in the night, wakes to the trap snapping. She thinks of the cavies and wonders how they will manage on their own, what Stanley will say when he returns and finds out she set them free, which may be the same as killing them. Her mother and father are in heaven, she reminds herself. They have gone to a better place, and she will one day join them there and apologize in person—not for the cavies but for ignoring the sirens. She digs into those words for comfort: *a better place.* But comes up empty, clenching her teeth. And when she prays she can't help but feel she is whispering to herself, which lends her prayers a level of desperation, or lunacy. If the soul carries on in heaven, why do these deaths feel so final, deep in her core, where her own soul apparently resides?

Because there is nothing after, she thinks, *there is only now.* But she never says this out loud.

When the end of the war comes, people laugh and sing, but there is no transition and Elsie is unprepared for the shift. All the foolish songs are meant to show a bravado she doesn't feel; their buoyancy is sickening. The words and the music insist on jubilance while the evidence of disaster sprawls around them. How do we clean it all up? Where do we begin?

"I think you need to stay with us," an auntie says—it doesn't matter which, because they come as a pair, like salt and pepper. Being with them only underscores her solitude. She is now a drifting fragment that needs to connect or risks endless loss in the atmosphere. And what of Stanley? Somehow she knows already, but returns home and waits.

Elsie sits in the window of the hat shop and looks out, marvelling at how things go back to normal, at how some things stayed normal all through the war. People get up in the morning and go whistling down the street, like characters in a movie. Weddings happen, there is even confetti. Babies are born and, around the corner, a frail old man falls down the stairs and suffers not even a bruise. Someone swears about burnt toast. Men and women come home after a harrowing time away, and many of them look the same as they did before, if you believe what their faces tell you. Richard Wilson is back, handsome as ever. More handsome, maybe, with broader shoulders and a confident gait. So not everyone has been altogether broken. On the streets of the partly obliterated neighbourhood, girls bump into him and say, *Oops, excuse me,* and he tips his hat and smiles with one side of his lovely mouth as he looks down at them. This is what they mean by those three simple words, *Life goes on.* You go with it or it goes on without you.

In the cellar Elspeth finds a nest of dead mice, babies without hair or teeth. At first they look like nine thumbs lying in a hatbox, they are that small. Their skin is criss-crossed, patterned like human skin, and she wonders if this is true for all animals when you take the fur away. For the cavies too.

For weeks there is no news of Stanley until the day a boy comes up the walk with a telegram. Angels of Death, they call these messengers. He was a little boy before the war, Elsie recognizes him from the neighbourhood, and she equates the lurch in her stomach with pity for him, that he has to do this awful job.

"I'm sorry," he says, and then again, "I'm sorry."

Has someone told him to say it twice?

He hands her the telegram and she notices the black dirt that fills his fingernails. He backs away and she stands watching him to make sure he doesn't trip and fall. When he's gone she opens the envelope. The sun beats down on her, as on the day she picked strawberries. A little crown swims at the top of the page.

DEEPLY REGRET TO REPORT THE DEATH OF YOUR SON PTE STANLEY LAHEY ON WAR SERVICE. LETTER TO FOLLOW.

But of course he is no one's son now. It is almost a relief to have the notice in her hands because it means she won't be faced with the task of telling him that all the cavies are gone; that their mother and father have died.

They died in the street. They were buried in rubble.

Why were they in the street? Why not the shelter, or the cellar at least?

I was picking berries. I didn't run back.

You mean they went looking for you.

I guess. I don't know. Yes.

There is good that comes out of their deaths, all three of them. They won't have to lay blame; they won't have to grieve for each other. They can leave all of that to her, just as they've left her their tangible things, each last scrap of paper and the tins of mixed nails and the delicate lavender sachets tucked into dresser drawers, a smell that lasts forever. Her father saved calendars every year since 1918, when the last war ended, but she has no idea why he kept them, or what she is meant to do with them now. There are no instructions as to how she should carry on. Everywhere in the store and the house above, piles of things form as she sorts like with like and examines the contents of her family's lives. Grateful for the burden, reluctant to reach the end to her task.

The sign on the door of the hat shop says closed, but the latch is unlocked, so whoever comes could enter on his own. She is near the back of the store, where the heads are, when she sees Richard Wilson through the glass. He cups his hands and peers in, but doesn't notice her. He only hesitates a moment or two before turning away. She watches him go, and sees an orange cat trot up to him and brush against his legs until he stops, stoops, and scratches its belly. He stands, and moves on.

Within days, James appears in his place. He comes out of nowhere and pulls open the door. He blinks three times when he sees her, then composes himself.

"I'm looking for a hat," he tells her. Then he smiles nervously and adds, "That sounds as if I've lost one but what I mean is I'm looking to buy one." He blushes. "For my mother. That is, if you have boxes. It has to travel a long way.

107

Do you have something blue?" He pauses, waiting for her response, and then laughs awkwardly. "The hat, I mean. Not the box. But the box can be blue too. It can be any colour."

He doesn't seem to notice the darkness around her, or else it doesn't scare him. Maybe he's seen too much already, but he doesn't look wise or jaded, or traumatized. He seems to have nothing to hide. In fact, in spite of his uniform, he looks as if he doesn't know there's been a war. She should tell him. But there's something about his face she doesn't want to spoil. The word that comes to mind is *open*. He's not a beautiful man, but there is something beautiful about him. She can feel the spiderwebs losing their grip on her, drifting back and up to the corners of the room.

In Elspeth's absence, we ate cheese sandwiches, popcorn, and marshmallow desserts. Dust balls floated across the floor and the white bathroom sink turned grey. Water spots flecked the mirror above, and the towels smelled sour, like wet animals. As I expected, my sleeves and pant legs grew shorter. My skirts inched toward my knees, and I was afraid that soon I would not be able to walk with my legs secretly bent to make myself look shorter. But James and I were happy enough. We gave each other all the space we needed to pursue our private interests, and if I wasn't following Suzy on my specialized bicycle—to our meadow, to our secret beach—I was alone in my room, thinking about her or me or the two of us together.

She had lived in thirteen places, she said. That was about one place for every year of her life, whereas my house had been a constant around me, and the town a constant around my house. When we were old enough, or perhaps sooner, Suzy and I might strap on backpacks and go travelling, the way our fathers had done in the war. I looked at the globe that sat on my dresser and gave it a spin, but there was something disorienting about my big hand hovering over the world—a sense that everywhere I went, the earth would be too small for me, and there was nothing I could do to change that fact.

At fourteen, Suzy was sure she was full-grown. She was already a little taller than her stout mother Margaret, but she reached only to my belly button, a cavernous hole that grew wider and deeper on a daily basis. I had never shown it to her, and I couldn't imagine I ever would, and yet the private places on my body weren't the ones that shamed me; the things that couldn't be hidden were worse by far: face, knees, elbows, hands, feet. Each so obviously like no one else's. My shoes would soon be too small, and I was hoping James would remember without me having to tell him that we needed to see the shoemaker.

He was keeping himself busy, putting the finishing touches on the home's renovations, painting doorframes dazzling white, polishing the glass of the skylights. He tried to decipher who he was without Elspeth, and he had to suppose that he had actually been without her for some time, even before she'd left. Still, he was amazed to realize how much she did for him without his noticing. She not only brewed his coffee in the morning, but she stirred in the milk and sugar too, and he felt resentful of the fact that he didn't even know how he liked it. One sugar or two? It was never quite the right colour without her. He decided she had—what was the word? *Infantilized* him. Or emasculated him. Either way, it wasn't good, it wasn't fair, it wasn't what he wanted.

He wished she could see that he was some sort of catch, because twice that first week, Iris—suit factory Iris, who also attended his Spanish class—sashayed up the walk, once with a fist full of flowers, and next with a still-warm dish she had cooked just for him.

"You'll be missing a woman of the house," she said coyly.

She lifted the lid and showed him the ham, pink like her skin, and for a horrible flash he saw himself rolling with her naked on the bed, and later he couldn't shake how the vision had had the clarity of a premonition. Unsettling, too, was the fact that Iris had cut her bangs between the first and second visit; they rose on an angle across her forehead with all the evidence of her intentions. Both times he accepted the gifts but didn't invite her in. He stood on the step with the container in his hands, and the warmth it exuded (like a body part) embarrassed him.

"Oh thank you. But really. You don't have to."

"Oh, I want to. I really do."

A sour powder smell moved past him as she waved her arm, and a foody whiff drifted from the dish in his hands.

"Yes. Well, thanks. Bye-bye." Nod, nod, his foolish head bobbing, his blushing body slinking indoors.

Even if Elspeth never returned, he believed he would never want anyone again. There was something peaceful about the thought of coming home, picking up a box of his beloved bite-sized Little Pleasures crackers on the way, and the rank cheese Elspeth detested, and just sitting nibbling those and some chocolate as the evening passed around him, like the man he'd seen in the apartment, who'd closed his blind to the world. And what was wrong with that? He had no great ambitions. He didn't need to be remembered; didn't need to make a mark. Why, then, the thrill at his next Spanish class when Iris sat down beside him and the smell of her perfume enveloped him? Spanish words were so romantic: *lavadero, legumbre, murmuro.* They worked the tongue and lips like a kiss did, and speaking them while Iris spoke them beside him made him feel like he was already cheating, bathed in sweat. Worse, Iris knew. He knew she knew.

So when she said, after class, "Why don't we walk together for a while? It's such a nice evening," he readily agreed, though it was hot and humid even after sundown. He trotted along beside her like a dog, embarrassed by the moon's brightness, its naked fullness, the shameful longing inside him, but not embarrassed enough to turn back. He had always been proud of the fact that he had never cheated, had rarely even lied to Elspeth, and up until now, even if he'd wanted to, even if he'd had the opportunity, he wouldn't have had the courage to cheat, and he believed that made him, in a roundabout way, a good man. But maybe it only proved that he was cowardly (as in Dieppe, and after). What if his whole life had been a sin of omission, a failure to act?

That was about to change—*he* was about to change it. He could feel his common sense slipping away as they stepped through the streets, feet moving in unison, as if dancing. Iris had blue shoes on, a little fancy but not overly so, and her fat feet looked swollen and sore. He saw himself pulling the shoes off, one then the other, and the intimacy of the imagined gesture sent a tickle across his sweaty chest. The summer breeze caressed them as they walked and brought the smell of the moist leaves and grasses, and just as he was

111

thinking he would be satisfied with this—a pleasant stroll with a friendly woman—they arrived at her door.

"Would you like to come in?" she asked. So simple, and so cliché.

For a moment he stood looking at her. Her curly hair was wild in the humidity and her cheeks glistened. She had close-together eyes, whereas Elspeth's were wide set, which gave her a wise, elegant appearance. Iris looked down. A line of blue eyeshadow had gathered in the crease of each eyelid. Her coated eyelashes were like spider legs. It occurred to him that he *wanted* to do something wrong. The fact that it was wrong made it all the more tempting. She blinked and looked up at him again, and, wordlessly, he accepted her invitation, stepping into a kind of fantasy land. Like a world made of candy.

Elspeth disliked sweets, he thought to himself as he removed his shoes. How could anyone dislike sweets?

He noticed the drapes with red and pink flowers, an orange sofa laden with pillows, a shelving unit cluttered with tacky souvenirs. On the wall was a framed photograph of Iris amid a sea of other uniformed women who'd served in the Canadian Women's Army Corps. His eye found her right away, in her tie and double-breasted jacket that strained at the buttons. She grinned out at him. He thought of asking her where she had served, but the question reminded him of his own treks through foreign lands and the tinnitus that haunted him for years afterwards—it would spoil the mood.

So, perched on the sofa with the pillows around him and a fan oscillating nearby, he accepted one and then another glass of wine as a Spanish record played in the background. The needle stayed at the end of the record, click-clicking, while he and Iris did what they knew they would do—the awful thing that could not be undone but felt so exquisite, even when he glimpsed his pale legs between hers, his dark socks still sealed to his feet, the clusters of purplish veins sprouting on her calves.

They sat on the sofa again, straightening their clothes, and the fan moved back and forth as if it was looking at him, then her, then him, then her, accusing. The heady feeling stayed with him, and it only evaporated as he walked home and realized that he had cheated two people rather than one. For it wasn't Iris who mattered to him. She might have been anyone, almost. All he needed from her was a certain level of desire that made him feel human again—but what kind of human was he, already regretting his act while at the same time knowing he would repeat it at the earliest opportunity?

When James arrived home after his encounter with Iris, I noticed nothing different about him. To me he was a father, nothing more or less; and to him I was a child. He couldn't tell that in the presence of my fragile new friend my ears rang louder and my head swooned. Who knew if that was normal or not? The ringing, I mean. Lately it was always there, but I still hadn't told anyone. Not the doctor or my parents, or even Suzy, though night and day she told me things.

Everything I learned about Suzy made me love her more.

The reverse had to be true as well, and so I began to confide my secrets, but slowly, one at a time. I said I would like to learn to fly a plane; that sometimes, just sometimes, my eyes ached and I didn't know why. *Do yours,* I wanted to ask— *Do you worry like I do?* But Suzy's stories were always more interesting than mine, and it was easier to listen than tell.

She hadn't always lived with her mother Margaret. Once, when she was about six years old and her mother was pregnant with Patrick, she was taken away by her Aunt Dodie, her mother's cruel sister; the morning before the drive, she ate a yard full of dandelions and threw up yellow in the back seat of the aunt's car.

"I thought eating them would bring me good luck," she admitted, "but it didn't."

Or maybe it had—because Suzy told me she'd escaped from the aunt's clutches on that very trip. They had stopped for gas. Aunt Dodie asked Suzy to come inside the store with her. She showed Suzy an array of sandwiches, asking her to choose one for lunch, but they were squishy and pink, the filling oozing out, and they made Suzy feel queasy. Suzy shook her head, stood near the door, and worried that now she would get nothing to eat.

Aunt Dodie rummaged in her purse and chatted with the man who owned the store, and Suzy watched the man's fat face, which shone with sweat though a fan blew on him and fluttered his tufts of hair. Suzy looked at the chocolate bars and then once more at Aunt Dodie and the man to be sure they weren't watching. She took a chocolate bar, slid it under her top, and then hurried out of the store. In the back seat of her aunt's car she tore off the wrapper and shoved the chocolate into her mouth, but it was too late. Her aunt was already returning to the car and saw as she opened the door. She grabbed Suzy's arm and pulled her out of the car.

"Did I not ask you if you were hungry?"

Suzy stood speechless with her mouth full of chocolate.

"I have paid that man for what you stole from him, and now I will wait here until you go in and apologize for your abominable behavior."

Hot and sick with shame, Suzy trudged toward the store. She pulled open the door and stepped in. The fan was blowing air into the space where the man was supposed to be standing, but there was no man there. Suzy glanced all around. She looked out into the parking lot and saw Aunt Dodie leaning against the car, wearing her sunglasses on her head like a movie star. She looked around the store again, down each aisle that teetered with dusty canned food and pop bottles, but she didn't see the man, so began to walk to the back of the store, where a door opened out to trees and more trees. Then she heard a toilet flush and, realizing the man would appear soon, she opened the door that led into the forest, and that was that—she ran.

"Weren't you afraid?" I asked.

"Of them catching me?"

"Well, yes, them too—but of the bees, I mean."

She looked confused for a moment, and then said, "Oh yeah. I wasn't allergic then." And went on with her story.

I thought, *But you were a baby that time you almost died. Can an allergy come and go?* I felt a weird foreboding, but abandoned it as she recounted her run through the woods, the coolness among the trees. I imagined myself running away, something I'd always wanted to do but I'd never had the courage. Plus, everyone would see me. There was not a place I could go where I wouldn't stand out from the rest, unless there really was a land of giants. But Suzy was lucky. She could slip undetected into the forest, and if I listened closely, I could go with her.

Birds and pieces of sky show through the branches above us as we run. We can't imagine a man so fat could keep up with us, nor our aunt in her high-heeled shoes and with her purse dangling from her wrist. But our dread hurries us on anyway. We run and trip until our own shoes come off. We keep going, and the worry of being bitten or stung by some forest creature just makes us faster, more nimble, and soon our feet barely touch the ground, which means we're almost flying.

Once more the forest opens and lets in the blue summer sky. We can see a meadow, and a farm beyond it. Tired now, and hungry, we walk toward the barn, hoping we might rest there unseen and steal something to eat. But as we draw closer we realize no one will be there, no one could possibly live in such a rundown place. The faded wood walls collapse in on themselves and the roof of every building on the property sags.

The sun is hot so we move into a shed to find shade. We sit on the hard dirt floor and cry, and then we stop crying because no one can hear us. Sunlight streams through a small, open door in the roof, and an old ladder is propped there. We stand at the bottom of the ladder and look up through the square in the roof. A flock of starlings flies by like a moving picture. It's hotter in the barn than outside. We put our hands and then feet on the rungs, and as we climb we wonder if we'll see Aunt Dodie running, or the man from the store, or maybe our mother, scanning the dandelion yard for us. Once we're through the opening we turn in a slow circle, but all we see is forest. Stepping out onto the roof, we look at our bare feet upon the soggy tiles, and just then there comes a great creak and groan beneath us, and the roof opens and we begin our fall.

"**I broke my arm in two places,**" Suzy said, as she stood and brushed bits of dried grass from her dress. "I have to be very careful with it now in case it happens again. It will always be my weak spot." She moved her arm so the elbow was close to her ear, and she waved it back and forth. "Sometimes I can hear it cracking," she said, bringing it next to my ear so I could hear the bones pop.

I didn't tell her, but there was no sound except the ringing that came from inside my head. But I treasured the fact that we had something in common, because my bones cracked too. They popped and snapped with the speed of my growing.

Suzy walked toward her bicycle and climbed on, and I realized this meant the story was done.

"But what then?" I asked. "What about your aunt and the shop owner and all that?"

I climbed on my bike and followed her, straining to hear her answer.

"Oh, I don't know. I went to live with her but after a while I went home again." She called back to me, "Want to ride to the train tracks?"

"Yes! Sure!" I rushed to catch up to her, to be close in case she fell and injured herself, or got chased by a deadly bee. She looked so small and vulnerable, riding ahead of me with her fine hair flying. And I, in this brief, wondrous time, had superhuman strength. Something was happening to me. My fatigue was gone—I had a new, strange energy. I could lift Suzy up and place her high in a tree; I could drape her over my shoulder and run with her. I'd hang from the railway bridge if she asked me. I'd never been so strong before, and it had to be Suzy who'd given me this new power. She could make the grass glow and the river sparkle. Everything changed in her presence, and I felt sorry for anyone who had no access to her vibrant world.

After spending the whole day with her, I spent it again in my memory, and sketched her image on pieces of paper I hid in my bedside drawer. *She said this and then I said that and then we laughed but what did she really mean by that,* and so on. I thought about Grace, who I'd also drawn, and my dressmaker's dummy, who had once been my closest friend, and I blushed at the idea of Suzy finding out about them, or seeing the drawings of her that could never do her justice. The embarrassment clung to me; were we so close that Suzy could read my mind? Nothing would be more awful than that: the person I wanted to know most knowing me in return.

The first time I stood in Suzy's doorway she had run inside to go pee. I was as big as the door, and must have looked foolish waiting there for her, bulk filling the frame, head drooping for a better look of the Malones' home. There were dried food splotches all over the stove. A bowl of wilty grapes, covered in fruit flies, sat on the unwiped kitchen table. The house smelled of cigarettes, a bit like Suzy's hair and clothes did, but stronger. I could hear the television, and through the archway into the living room I could see Patrick's dirty feet on the coffee table. Then something tickled my legs, and I let out a little scream before realizing it was a cat coming in from outside. It wrapped around my ankles, rubbing and purring. Patrick appeared too—he must have heard me—and when the cat started to walk into the kitchen, I gripped the doorframe to steady myself, reached forward, and scooped her up.

"Sorry, I guess I shouldn't be standing here with the door open."

"It's okay," said Patrick. "That's our cat." As though to make conversation, he added, "She has kittens too."

The cat jumped from my arms and looked back at me, and I noticed the black ring around her eye, and another around her twitching tail. She fit the description of the cat Suzy said her mother had abandoned outside of town, a cat with kittens. So the cat had found them? Or they had found her? I pictured the cat journeying along the roadside with her trail of kittens behind her, showing up on the front step and demanding to be cared for. Why wouldn't Suzy have told me? I eased myself down to crouching and put my hand out, and the cat came to me and sniffed my fingers.

"What's her name?" I asked.

"Dodie." Patrick grinned and his pointy ears moved a little with the change in expression.

"Oh. Like your aunt? You named her after your aunt?"

He gave me a weird look and the smile faded. "We don't have any aunts. Only an Uncle Mo."

I was already tallying up the reasons for the misunderstanding. The aunt had been so cruel that Patrick, who was younger than Suzy, hadn't ever met her. And maybe the cat was really old. She had been named long ago, before the aunt revealed her cruelty. Did old cats have kittens? I was sure they did. I almost asked, *How old is Dodie?* but I decided I didn't want to know, so instead I said, "I'll just wait outside for Suzy—will you tell her?"

Patrick nodded yes. He watched me stand again, to my full height, and looked at me with wonder. He had hair the same suntanned colour as his skin, shorn close so that the bug bites showed around his elf ears. As I stood beneath the big maple tree between our houses, I could see him peering out at me, and I knew in my bones that he would always remember this moment. Perhaps it would grow in his memory, a giant under a tree outside his window.

I didn't say anything to Suzy. We got on our bikes and went to the beach, as usual, but as we rode the questions tangled inside me. The yellow string on my handlebars glowed. When had the cat come back? Or was this a different one, with identical markings, and what if Dodie had been an aunt by marriage, is that what Patrick meant when he said we don't have any aunts, that they didn't have any *real* aunts? Did Uncle Mo have a wife? The aunt, the cat, the kittens, the aunt, the cat, the kittens, everything else was pushed away by this new and strange information. I didn't even realize until we got there that Suzy had ridden to the main beach instead of the secluded place we always went to together, and when she stopped and I pulled up beside her, she said, "I was getting sick of that old, pebbly place. This is *way* better."

She sounded just like herself, but her face startled me. I looked at her and realized I didn't know her, and seeing the mask slip gave me the scariest feeling. The eyes, the nose—everything was the same, but different. Then she smiled at me, and the feeling was gone. The doubts and the questions had gnarled themselves into a tight ball that could be tucked away and ignored.

I parked my bike, took the towel from my basket, and followed her onto the sand. There were lots of people at the beach. It was late summer, and everyone was soaking up the last of it before school began again. The sun sparkled on the dark water, and on the other side of the river a canoe passed. I thought of that day with James, the great blue heron nodding at me, and for an instant I wished myself back to that time, even though I was sure I was happier now, with Suzy.

We spread our towels and Suzy took off her sundress to reveal the red swimsuit beneath. She had small breasts and a waist that curved in like a woman's. I hadn't yet grown in any of the places that counted, though I waited for that with a mix of dread and excitement, wondering how it might change me on the inside. Under my jumper I had shorts and a top only—I hadn't swum for years, as I was afraid of tripping and falling, that no one would be able to lift me. But I remembered the feeling of weightlessness, the silken water on my skin. Suzy loved the water. At our spot downriver, she sometimes stayed under for a long time, and I'd stand on the shore with the water lapping my toes, looking for bubbles on the surface. *Where did she go—what would I do if....* And then she'd shoot up and shout, "Scared you!"

There was some comfort in the people around, and the lifeguard sitting in his tall chair with his whistle and his life preserver ready. If something happened, someone else would be able to save her. Yet I preferred our private beach, full of rocks and trees, and sharp pine needles that poked out of the sand. Here I kept my shoes on because of the people rather than the pine needles. And as I removed my jumper I could feel the stares that burned hot as the sun.

Haven't seen her at the beach in ages.
Where would she get a suit to fit? See—she doesn't have one.
Would you come to the beach if you looked like that?
Don't sit in her shadow if you want a suntan.
Who's that girl with her?
Ratty hair!
Pretty though. Pretty girl.

I cared more for Suzy than myself, but Suzy didn't seem to notice anyone staring, not even the brown-haired boy, David, who walked three circles around us before wandering down the beach. He was a grade ahead of me, but I knew who he was. He had dark, deep-set eyes, a pale gash for a mouth. His nose grew straight up into his forehead, like a lion's. He was actually a striking boy, with broad, tanned shoulders and a lanky frame. He moved stealthily, barely lifting his feet from the sand. There was something awful about such a fluid gait.

Soon I had blocked out everyone, and Suzy was burying me in sand. She had made a hollow for me, and I moved into it and lay face up as she poured more sand over me. It took a mountain to cover my body, and the little grains rolled over my skin like minuscule people running this way and that.

Suzy was humming a song that played every day on the radio that year, and the sleepier I got the more her voice sounded like fine chimes, far away. The parts of me that were covered in sand were refreshingly cool, but my face stayed warm from the sun above me. I could feel my eyes drooping closed, fluttering open, drooping again.

I don't know how long I slept, but when I woke, my face felt tight and burned. I looked at the sky and saw how the cloud pattern was just like sand drifting, as if the sky reflected what it saw below. If I looked long enough I might find myself up there, and Suzy. But where was Suzy? Sand scuttled through my hair as I lifted myself up to my elbows. I saw her down by the shore, squatting near the water and writing something in the wet sand with a stick. I was about to call out when I saw David approach her. He walked over whatever she was writing, and she stood and kicked water at him. Was she laughing? She bent again to write, and again he trod on it. When she stood this time, lifting her foot, he grabbed it, and there she was, hopping, completely at his mercy. I sat straight up and the sand poured off me.

Had she put her hair up? Before it was hanging down, with just a hair band to hold it back. It had tickled my face when she'd poured the sand over me. But now it was up in a loop at the back, loose pieces escaping.

David let go of her foot and kicked water back, and she ran splashing into the river. But he was right behind her. The water rose to their knees and their hips, and then they dove in, swimming deeper. I listened for voices carrying off the water, but the ringing in my ears took over and I couldn't hear what they were saying. I pushed myself up to standing, woozy from lack of food and heat. My belly rumbled, and out of habit I put my hand over it to muffle the humiliating sound.

A scream from Suzy. She ducked under and I held my breath, but then she splashed up again. Did she see me? Would she wave? The sand burned my feet as I walked across it, huge strides, giant leaps. I could feel my hands throbbing, my big legs rubbing together, my cheeks wobbling. Even my breath was loud and large. My stomach gurgled again, and the noise brought tears to my eyes, but I was moving forward regardless. The ground was shaking with my every step, and then I was at the water's edge and I glanced down to see what she had written, but David and Suzy's footsteps combined had erased the words. The certainty that those words had been about me didn't stop me from following Suzy into the water, shoes and all. I kept imagining myself falling and not being able to stand, and Suzy running to save me, the water travelling up my nose and into my mouth and me choking and spluttering. There was something so compelling about being helpless. And it would be tragic and she would lean over me crying, and understand how much she loved me.

The water was up to my knees and then my hips, and my shorts were floating out from my body. My shoes were full, my T-shirt was drifting. Had she seen me yet, did she see me coming? She kept dipping under and letting her toes emerge, pointed, and then her two naked feet, and David would grab them and pull them and then her head would pop up, but she was never facing me, so how could I know if she was happy or not?

It was only when I reached her that I realized I was crying. Tears were dripping down my face, but they might have been water, no one could really say.

"Ruth!" said Suzy. "What's wrong?" She had a half-smirk, a kind of *you fool* incredulous look that made a barrier between us. She glanced at David and back at me. "What are you doing?"

"Are you okay?" I asked. I knew how ugly I looked when I cried. "I just wanted to make sure you were okay."

"Whoa," said David, "is this your bodyguard?"

Suzy laughed. "Jeez, Ruth—relax. I'm not exactly drowning." She dove under again, and her two white feet appeared and disappeared, fish jumping.

I stood looming over David and Suzy. The water came to her chin, his shoulders, but I was only half-immersed, and shivering. It crossed my mind that if what she'd written and erased had been about me, it was ridicule, but if it had been about him, it was teasing. I forced a laugh and said something strange, like, "I fell asleep, I think I was dreaming," and then I turned and walked through the water with leaden steps.

On the beach, the sand caked my shoes, and I could hear Suzy and David laughing behind me. But I stayed and stayed. Such a long afternoon. When I lay back, the clouds made a magnificent show, bordered by the maples and poplars behind me whose leaves moved with the wind. The wind would be my favourite thing, if I ever had to choose. The trees were giants spreading their arms wide, loving the breeze.

I was quiet on the way home. Lightheaded and sunburned. I felt sorry that my shoes were ruined. The leather would be hard now, and brittle, and I knew the shoes had cost a lot of money. I thought of Elspeth and felt guilty. I had seen her sneering from the picture window the day Suzy moved in. And then my memory tripped on something else

127

from that afternoon: how I had stood grinning at my new friend as chairs had drifted by in the background; a floor lamp had sauntered past; and in a cardboard box, kittens had been mewling.

Why would someone lie about things that didn't matter?

❦

Lies were on James's mind too. He had to push them out in order to get any sleep at all in the pink room, where the wedding photograph watched him. He thought about plunking it face down but couldn't bring himself to do so, mostly because he feared forgetting to prop it up again and the questions that might bring when Elspeth arrived home. She was in his thoughts more than ever, and in a tender way—and yet he somehow had the ability to banish her from his mind for a blissful pocket of time when Iris presented herself, or when he (yes, he had done so, in the manner of a peacock or a great moose) presented himself right back. To the pink room he whispered an apology that finally helped him sleep, but he would have remained wide awake, agonizing, had he known that in England, Elspeth thought of him as often, was even surprised by the way she talked to him in her head, saying things she wouldn't say if he was with her.

She remembered their first few dates, the rapid escalation of their courtship, and their goodbye when he was shipped home. Then her own arrival on his family's doorstep as he gripped her elbow. All of them with the same open look James had: the brother Norm, his perky wife Tess, the father, the mother. There was a newness, a luckiness about them that was both off-putting and refreshing. The mother had worn her blue hat for the occasion, though it was not a hat meant to be worn indoors, and Elspeth felt embarrassed that she didn't know. The hat was at an awkward angle as well—and it reminded Elspeth of the hat shop she had left behind.

In the kitchen, she stood with the mother and mashed carrots wearing a borrowed apron, and the woman, a stranger, really, said, "You should call me Mother, Elspeth. We're family now." Which, kind as it was, brought to mind all that she had lost that could never be replaced. The attempt at intimacy had failed, because in avoiding calling James's mother Mother, she didn't call her anything at all in subsequent years, except in letters and Christmas cards—*Dear Mother*—and even then it felt like a silent betrayal of her real mother, who had doused herself in powder after each bath so that her skin had a ghostly quality, a smell of primrose. Elspeth still longed to believe in ghosts; the wish for their existence came between her and living people.

Elspeth had arranged the aunts' funeral in England. She had seen Bea and Franny laid to rest side by side in an old, crowded cemetery full of higgledy-piggledy tombstones, beside the graves of her mother and father. She had always meant to secure proper markers for her parents, but she had never done so, and Franny and Bea had eventually taken care of things after she'd left. Her brother was buried on foreign soil, among columns of white stones that were in a way like soldiers, but she had never visited his grave. Now would be the time. Buy a ticket, board a train. But as on the day of the strawberries, she felt unable to move. And there were Franny and Bea's things to take care of, and their flat to empty so that someone else could move in. It was too late for a visit to Stanley to make any meaningful difference.

For several days in a row, at the beginning of her trip, she'd gone through the aunts' belongings and tried to sort things into neat piles of what she could keep, what she could donate, and what she could throw away. She was reminded of that flat space of time after the war, before James had come, when she'd sorted the belongings of her mother, father, and brother. The minutiae of a life was staggering. Hair clips and shoehorns and jars of buttons and pencil holders and clip-on earrings and souvenir spoons and fancy teacups with saucers and embroidered linens and embroidery thread and half-used balls of wool and crochet hooks and dresses and shoes and underpants and slips and insoles and nail clippers and powder puffs—on and on it went. The pile of things she wanted to keep grew large on the first day, but then became smaller and smaller, until the only things left were photographs, a fold-up plastic kerchief for rainy days, and a watch she felt sure had been her mother's. She slipped it on and wound it, and saw how her hand, wrist, and arm had become like her mother's, elegantly shaped, but patterned by the fine lines of aging.

Her mother had seemed so old in that last year of the war, but in actuality she had not been much older than Elspeth was now. Bea, though, had lived nearly to eighty, and Franny to eighty-one, fair and worthy ages, and so their deaths, blessedly together, should have been an easy loss compared with the others. Yet now and then in the aunts' small space, which still smelled of life, Elspeth gasped as though the floor had opened and she was falling. Franny and Bea were her last connection with the past; her family had withered to a close, and she was here to sweep up the remnants.

One day she came upon a box of letters. She recognized her own handwriting on the pale blue envelopes, and saw that the dates ranged from the year she went to Canada right up to last year's Christmas card. Each one had been saved and kept in order, though they offered so little.

No, please don't think of coming. The baby is healthy, and we're really doing just fine, and I know the trip would be too much for you. Much as I'd love to see you. James's mother comes some weekends and has been an absolute wonder.

Then later on:

Ruthie is growing like a weed! I'm sending along a snap of her in a new dress I made, but she grows out of them so quickly I can hardly keep up.

And later still:

I know it's been ages since I sent a photo of Ruthie. I must get organized and send something soon or you just won't know her anymore. No, please don't think of coming. The trip would be so tiring for you and the summers here are stifling. We'll get there one of these years, I promise you that. James is itching to return to England.

That wasn't true, really. He had mentioned England on occasion, though only for her sake. And it had been easy to make the argument that they couldn't afford to travel. Elspeth hated the thought of her worlds merging. In the early years especially she had missed her aunts and her home, but what she missed most was the time before the war, which could not be revived by visiting. Plus there was the question of the huge, unexplainable daughter. Never Ruthie for Elspeth, as the letters claimed, but Ruth. Missing was easier than interacting. Sooner or later, missing went away, so you really could bottle things up until they lost all their potency.

131

Days later with Suzy, everything was forgiven, almost forgotten. We were on our bicycles and the breeze was sneaking through a slit I'd made in each shoe, right at the toe, to relieve the pressure. The coolness on my hot feet was wonderful, and anyway the shoes had already been spoiled by that other day at the beach, so what was the harm in cutting them, just a little bit, if I had outgrown them?

As we rode along the south bank of the river, Patrick followed. We crossed the first bridge, then rode along the north bank to the school. That old nervousness wormed into my belly when the building came into view. It was red brick, old-fashioned, with a bell tower and big windows through which light streamed into the classrooms. Suzy dropped her bike and ran over, looking into the basement windows. She had never been inside the school but in a couple of weeks she'd be a student here, and I could picture her standing with her books in the crook of her arm, chatting so easily with the others as they flocked around her. I didn't relish the day I would have to share her, but I gripped her waist and lifted her up to my height so she could look through the upper windows. Reflected in the glass, I could see Patrick behind us in the playground, doing wheelies on his bicycle. We looked in every window, one at a time, and I noticed how Suzy held her body stiffly, how she studied each space with a solemn expression. It surprised me to think she might be afraid when she was always so sure of herself, so brash and brave. I felt a surge of protectiveness—of confidence. The image of me creeping to school along the back lanes, dreading every encounter, seemed more like a scene from a movie than a memory. I had reason now, and purpose, and someone to walk with. We could go together. I set Suzy down and leaned close to her.

"It'll be okay, you know."

She looked up at me. The vulnerability vanished with a roll of her eyes and a sputtered breath. "What are you talking about, Ruth?"

It was her idea, on the way back, to take the second bridge instead of the first. She pointed ahead, saying, "Let's cross here," and then we turned and saw it right away, stretched across the road in large letters:

GIANT SLUT

RUTH B. LOVES DAVID M.

We both stopped riding, and stood looking at the words. I felt so dizzy I thought I would fall over. Suzy got off her bike and leaned it against the railing. She waited as a car passed, and then walked over to where the words were written and tried to rub them out with her shoe, but the letters stayed clear.

"Oh, Ruth," she said. "Who would do this?" She didn't look at me. She kept her head down, and her feet worked furiously.

I tried to make myself get off my bike as well, to put my big feet over the words and scuff them, but I couldn't move. A sick feeling started in my stomach, and spread all through me. Even when Patrick appeared and poured his last bit of pop on the letters in a failed attempt to wash them away, I kept staring at the back of Suzy's head, and the tangle of hair that had been there even the day before. I kept staring and staring until my eyes stung. We were standing close enough that I could reach over, grab the knotted mass of hair, pick her up, and drop her in the river. I closed my eyes to unthink the thought, and then I looked up to the sky to see if there were clouds that might release a great, cleansing rainfall, but the sky was blue. It was wide and clear, just like that day with the red balloon, when I was small and my parents towered over me.

I am at a fair with giant pumpkins and cotton candy, animals brought from a farm. The pig's nostrils perfect circles as on a telephone dial. A man on stilts sails past, with striped pants that make him taller still. He grips the strings to a bunch of balloons that stretch up to the sky. Something makes his eye catch me. I see him looking around and then finding me, smiling with his painted mouth—the real grin under the false one. He pulls a balloon loose, the way you pick a flower from a bouquet, and his gloved hand delivers it down to me. His thumb and finger pinch the string, and his other fingers spray up in the manner of a lady drinking tea. He raises his eyebrows, blinks and nods, and then he's off with long strides, pant legs flapping. Tiny head with a hat tied on. I'm left holding the balloon, clutching the string with a sweaty hand, and mouthing *thank you*. Elspeth and James keep fussing with the string, trying to wrap it around my wrist and tie it, but I won't let go. I squeeze my fingers shut, and my sharp, little nails dig into my palm. The balloon is fat and shiny—it bobs and sways above me. I want Elspeth and James to stop talking, stop touching the string and making the balloon jerk this way and that. I love the red against the blue sky. We keep wandering. We look at a donkey with droopy eyes and stand in front of a pyramid of jarred preserves. I sit on the back of a pony as it walks around in a circle with other ponies carrying other children. James walks beside us, and Elspeth claps from the sidelines, calling out to me and waving, but I'm not listening. I'm watching the balloon dance to the clomp of the pony's hooves. When the ride ends and I'm lifted off the pony's back and set down on the ground, the string slips from my hand, just like that. James grabs for it, grabs again and again as the balloon rises, but it's too late—the balloon sails up. I can see it for a long time but I know it will never come back to me.

Summer was closing. The stink of the pulp and paper mill mixed with the fragrance of early September, the smell of leaves dying, of old, dry grass. Such a complicated smell of hope and longing and fear. The bugs were fat and lazy, and the happy pink cosmos flowers were shrivelling and going to seed. I knew, seeing the casual manner in which Suzy brushed away bees, that she was far from allergic, but I felt only relief, and maybe some small sense of bruising. It didn't matter that she had lied if her life was no longer in danger. Or even if it had never been in danger. Whatever purpose her lies served, I felt sorry for her for needing them.

She needed me, too. That was the important thing. At first I thought I was dreaming when she appeared beside my bed one night, shaking me and hissing, "Get up! Hurry! My mom has fallen!" And in my nightgown made from an old sheet, I threw off my covers and flew behind her, barefoot across the floor and out through the garden. I didn't even think about whether or not James could see me from his bedroom window, where a light was still glowing. We rushed across the lawn, into the house that was full of silence, as if the rooms were holding their breath. We ran down the hall past Patrick's room, and I glimpsed him there, standing near the door, eyes shining.

From the top of the basement stairs we could see Suzy's mother sprawled near the bottom step. She had been carrying laundry down, and it was strewn on the floor around her. Her eyes were closed; she was still. Suzy grabbed my arm and pulled me downstairs. My head grazed the ceiling. I had no time to turn my big feet sideways on the steps, and my heels plunked down. It seemed impossible that I didn't fall too, and barrel right over Suzy at the moment she needed me most.

Suzy's face was blotched from crying as she crouched beside her mother. But I saw Margaret's chest rise and fall, and I knew she was alive. I could smell alcohol—bitter and tangy—and, as always, the pungent nicotine smell that permeated their clothes and surroundings.

"We should call an ambulance," I said.

"No!" said Suzy. Then, more gently, "She just needs to be in bed."

Suzy stroked her mother's face, tucked the coarse blonde hair behind Margaret's ear the way a mother would do for a child.

"I can't wake her up," Suzy said. "Will you lift her? Please?"

I stood there, hanging above them. I sensed someone behind me and turned to see Patrick at the top of the stairs. Blue airplane pyjamas that bagged out at the knees. Frayed collar. Everything here was coming apart at the seams. They knew it too, but not how to stop it.

"I should get my father."

"Ruth—please! Will you help us or not?"

Though bending was hard for me, I got myself down and slid my arms beneath Margaret, and I thought of those powerful weightlifters as I rose with her. Flexing every muscle, lifting from my core. I had never been strong until Suzy arrived. My bulk had been a useless thing. Now I could do anything she asked.

Arms shaking, I carried Margaret stair by stair, Patrick leading the way down the hall, Suzy behind. I stepped through more dirty clothes on the floor of Margaret's bedroom, and laid her in her unmade bed. As I was pulling away, her eyes opened and looked at me. She had the ragged look of a survivor—someone who keeps surviving in spite of herself.

As I crossed the lawn to go home, Patrick called to me from his open window. I turned, but couldn't see him in the darkness.

"Thank you," he said.

I raised my hand to him as his curtains drifted closed.

139

I couldn't get back to sleep that night. What if Margaret's back had been broken, or her neck? What if moving her had been the absolute wrong thing to do? If I found out I'd killed her, what would I do?

In the morning I rushed over and rapped on the door, but Margaret herself answered, squat body wrapped in a dingy pink robe, bobby pins at her temples. Bacon sizzled in a pan.

"Suzy's still sleeping," she said in her raspy voice. "Sleeps till goddamn noon if I let her."

She seemed to know nothing of the night before, and there was no sign that anything had been broken or bruised. She motioned for me to come in and crossed the kitchen floor in her bare feet. Her toenails were painted bright red and looked just like candies.

"Suzy!" she hollered. "Suzy!!" Without turning from the grease popping in the pan, she said, "Just go ahead in Ruth. You'll need a foghorn to get her moving."

I entered the hall down which I had carried Margaret the night before, folding her into a deep v so that her head and feet would not scrape along the walls. It was odd to be here again in the daytime, and see how things had reverted to normal. I opened the door to Suzy's room and sat on the bed beside her. Her eyes moved under her eyelids and I wondered what she was dreaming about. Me? The fall? Or David?

When she woke up, she wasn't surprised to see me there. She just looked at me in that flat way she sometimes did, which locked me out. I couldn't get at her, but couldn't keep myself from trying.

"I'm glad your mom's okay," I whispered.

She rolled over so I couldn't see her face, and I put my head on the pillow beside her.

"Why do you always wear your hair like that?" she asked, still not turning to me. "It doesn't look very good on you."

I pulled the elastic from my hair and asked, "What would look better?" Whatever she wanted, I'd give her. Nothing was too much to ask.

***

Elspeth had been away three weeks but would return home within days. She would scrub the sinks and the floors and do the mounds of laundry, washing out the evidence of her absence. Once the stolen moments had slipped down the drain, everything would be clean, as it once was. She wanted and needed to clean things, both at home and in England.

When she'd emptied the aunts' flat, Elspeth swept and mopped it, and set to washing away all trace of Franny and Bea. The cleaning soothed her, and there was time to do it properly, whereas at home there were so many other chores, and work on top of them. She did it all, but mostly felt that she did nothing well, and the disappointment plagued her. All her life she'd been atoning for something, making amends, but even the amends didn't seem good enough.

On the shelf above the bathtub she found an array of strange, squiggly marks blackening the wood. She scrubbed and scrubbed, but they would not be erased. She covered them with a dusting of harsh cleansing powder, resolving to return to them later, and went about washing the bathroom floor. Beneath a loose tile she discovered a cluster of bobby pins, one still holding a strand of grey hair. Elspeth stood and rubbed away a bit of the cleanser so she could see the squiggles again, and as she laid a bobby pin down on the matching stain, she closed her eyes, for the image of Bea sinking back in the tub was so strong now that it brought tears to her eyes. She blew the powder away, and let the fossils remain.

Every day when she left the aunts' flat to pick up food for her simple meals, she travelled along Cockspur Street, not knowing she was walking in the 250-year-old footsteps of Irish giant Charles Byrne.

He was one in a long line of giants who showed themselves for money. When he first got to England from Ireland, he was a twenty-one-year-old man embarking on what he was sure would be a bright future. Newspaper advertisements reported that he could be seen in an elegant apartment next to Cox's Museum. The Living Colossus, they called him, or the Wonderful Irish Giant; he measured eight feet, two inches. The nobility and the faculty of the Royal Society hurried to see him, and claimed despite his grey complexion and chronic cough that he was more impressive than any natural curiosity ever offered to the public. They said his address was singular and pleasing, his person truly shaped and proportioned to his height, and that the sight of him was more than the mind could conceive, the tongue express, or the pencil delineate.

From 11:00 until 4:00 he would stand there, letting them look at him, and his loathing for them grew by the hour. A woman whispered to her companion, "He isn't as tall as they say," and the fellow's cruel eyes travelled down the length of him, as if measuring by glance. Charles's feet ached and his brain hummed with boredom, though he composed rude poems to amuse himself. Sometimes the onlookers engaged him in conversation, and asked silly questions such as "How is it that you came to us all the way from Ireland?" And he would answer, "Well, I just felt an urge, and so I stepped across." They would titter politely, but they did not take kindly to the dead look in his eyes, made deader each night at his favourite pub, as he drank himself into numbness.

Not far from where Charles Byrne teetered on his barstool, the eccentric surgeon John Hunter was steadily building his impressive collection of specimens. Little people and big ones were particularly intriguing. And this was the age, after all, of bodysnatchers. Hunter hired one to approach Charles and offer a tempting sum to will his body to the doctor after death. Which would be soon enough, judging by Charles's constant hacking and the yellowed whites of his eyes. But Charles recoiled and turned the offer down. The man appeared in the crowd the next day and the next, staring at him from amid a sea of faces.

Charles's paranoia grew; he drank more, and finally quit showing himself. He had always trusted in the idea that even if his body perished his soul would live on, no matter what happened to him, but he had begun to doubt that that was the case, because already, while he was still living, he could feel his soul withering away. He wandered the streets in the wee hours, when few would notice him, and as he drifted by the upper windows he peered in longingly at regular people asleep in their regular beds. When he returned to his quarters he wanted only to sleep as they slept, but his dreams were marred by nightmares of his own demise, and his soul displayed as a physical thing. Stuffed and shellacked.

Once he began to cough blood, he made arrangements with some of his pub friends to promise, when the time came, that they'd place him in a lead coffin and dump him in the Thames, where no one could get at his remains. But somewhere along the line his plan was stymied. A handful of years after his death, when the publicity had quelled, a giant skeleton appeared in Hunter's museum, encased in gleaming glass, the brown bones indicating a hasty boiling. And so the giant endured in Elspeth's time, though she had no knowledge of him. He stood surrounded by skulls and bones and lizards in jars, an elephant's see-through skeleton, and thousands of birds and animals whole or in pieces. Insect mouthparts and human teeth, coiled intestines, parasitic worms, and the delicate frames of woodpeckers. Wondrous things to be gawked at into eternity. Things that had to be seen to be believed.

Elspeth thought she had read about all the giants—the one with no heart in his body, the one with the beanstalk, and so on. But she had never looked outside of storybooks, into the lives of actual giants. It hadn't occurred to her that my condition was a condition. Her cache of giant legends was still tucked away in her half of the closet, disappointing because it had never offered what she'd sought: stories that might comfort me, or her, or all of us. Just as I did, for a long time she entertained the belief that once there had existed a race of giants. But she was not one for delusions. Even the bible made her uneasy in that regard, which was why she had to pray so fiercely. In the end all the evidence told her that there had never been a race of giants. That giants have always come to us one by one. Rare, organic blunders pressed into a dollhouse world.

With Franny and Bea put to rest, Elspeth travelled by bus and train, having no particular destination in mind, zigzagging up to Liverpool, then over to Wales and on down the coast. When it drizzled, she took the little rain kerchief out of her bag, unfolded it, and tied it on. She felt just like an old lady, sensible and prepared, and she remembered the handbags Franny and Bea had carried, with a special compartment for everything. The decisive sound of them snapping shut indicated that everywhere, everything would be okay.

When your purse is clean, your mind is clear.

One of them had said that, but she couldn't remember which. That sort of tidiness was what she'd strived for in her own life, in every aspect, but she could never achieve it, nor let go of the fierce desire to do so. And James: so accommodating, so infuriating. *The house looks clean to me. I'd love you even if it were filthy.* Grinning and wiggling his eyebrows. He had never really appreciated who she really was—he had never even tried to understand her.

On through Wales, she couldn't absorb herself in the scenery, and it rolled by in a green haze or a blue wash, depending. Once in a while she moved back in time to a moment in her childhood, but she could never tell why or what she might learn from the memory, for each time it was only the simplest thing: herself in bare feet finding seashells; or staring up at the hornets' nest under the eaves outside her bedroom window—waiting and waiting for something to happen, like now. It struck her that a memory was different than a recollection, since a memory just came, unbidden, and a recollection was something you sought out; you invited it back. And then she tried to choose which moments she would invite back, and to *recollect* the details, but precious little would come. The day that James arrived. The day she gave birth. Those events were always somewhere in her mind, camouflaged by current worries.

Sometimes she left the bus or train on a whim, and just walked. In the countryside she came upon a house entangled in weeds. It startled her at first to think that she might be trespassing on someone's property, but then she noticed the tattered curtains that blew through the window, where there was no glass. The front door of the house hung crooked from the top hinge. She drew closer. Through the window in what must have been the living room she could see a stained mattress with the stuffing spilling out, and just beyond it a doll's head, parted from the body. Nearby was a heap of everything: an old soup tin, toy trucks and cars, pantyhose, cereal boxes, a tube of toothpaste, and half of a game board. She had the impression that someone had swept it all into a pile, but couldn't be bothered to dispose of it, and it made her think of the Malones' house next door, of Margaret and Suzy, who she despised, and of Patrick, who was still young enough to escape blame for the way he was.

But then it seemed to her that her own house was in similar disarray; perhaps this was how she'd left things when she'd flown away. It was how the aunties' place looked when she'd finished with it, and how the rooms above the hat shop appeared to her in her memory the day she'd turned her back on them, despite the fact she knew she had scrubbed the floors and the walls in both places until her hands turned pink; she had left both places so empty that her footsteps echoed through the rooms as she walked away. She could never do enough. She peered into the abandoned house again. The walls were covered in tiny pink flowers. There were nails there, and brighter squares where pictures had been. So, in with the things left behind, there were traces of what had been taken.

On her way back to London, the train stopped at her little town, which had not quite been swallowed up by the city. There was nothing to do but get off, even though the act of doing so made her nauseous. Heart fluttering, feet on home ground, she thought of Richard Wilson moving toward her on the cobblestones. The rippled clay roof tiles and the enormous plane trees with their arms outstretched made her ache for a time she'd never admitted to missing. She was home. An excruciating, beautiful pain came over her with every step she took. It poured over her like buckets and buckets of water rushing down, but no one seeing her would ever guess she was feeling anything unusual. She approached the hat shop—now a bakery—the way anyone might, as if she had no connection to the place other than her human need for bread. She grasped the door handle, palm tingling, and pushed open the door, breath held with the hope or fear that one might enter the past so easily. She herself had hung the bell to the door jamb, and well knew the sound it made each time the door opened—hadn't it rung that way when Stan had come home, and when she'd left for the strawberry field, and then again when James had appeared, looking for something blue? Sounds were like smells; they snuck up on you and triggered memories, wanted or not.

The old floor had been painted, but was made up of the original wood planks, and there was the square trap door that led down to the cellar. It looked like an empty picture frame in the floor. If she lifted the door now she might see the ladder steps and the crumbling concrete walls, and her mother and father there waiting, wringing their hands. *Elsie, where have you been?*

The little door remained closed, and the place was almost unrecognizable. Customers chatted and sipped tea at pretty round tables that held vases of daisies. Loaves of bread sat where the heads used to be. She stood in line, looking as normal as she could, but when asked for her order she was speechless.

"Ma'am, I said what would you like?"

Silence.

"Ma'am?"

Like a crazy woman she backed away, feeling for the door handle behind her, bumping into strangers and making her way out with the bell clanging.

Near the end of Elspeth's weeks away, the little jar of deodorant had been wiped clean, and James was perspiring more than ever. He tried to tell himself that this was only because it was hot out, and his postal suit was dark and heavy. But the sweat gushed out of him even on weekends, after he'd showered and put on his light summer clothes—the seersucker shirt that made him think of nurses in the war. He was effusing guilt, especially in his dark, private areas, and he felt convinced that Elspeth would come home and smell his guilt the minute she walked in the door. She could always tell when something had gone off in the fridge, even with the fridge door shut, and from down the hall she knew when he had failed to close the lid to the laundry hamper, his dirty socks stinking on top of the heap. And how would he answer, how would he defend himself once the accusation had been made? He knew he wouldn't, that he was too much of a coward for anything more than denial. But the lie would rot his insides.

Worse was when he thought of Elspeth returning to work at the suit factory, and spending her days with Iris, whom he understood now was exceptionally fragile, and therefore dangerous and unpredictable—the enemy, no less. And every day the trepidation would be with him as he came home from work, waiting to find out if Iris had said something to Elspeth about their affair. (Could it be called an affair? He was new to the realm of adultery, and didn't know if three times counted as such, but it seemed important to name the thing in his mind. To *end* it, yes, but also to define it.) He didn't know if he could live with the constant worry of *did she already know, would she find out tomorrow.* He doubted he was strong enough.

And if he *could* tell her, was it asking too much of her to forgive him?

Life was not unlike war, he decided. There was the constant need to protect, defend. Confusion regarding the enemy, and from which direction they might attack. Chaos when the rulebook was lost or illegible, and one had to make one's own way through the battle, without specific commands from superiors. Only once before had his own weaknesses been so acutely apparent to him, and inwardly he underscored the fact that he had gotten through that other time, thus he would come through this one too. But the realization felt nothing like a light at the end of a tunnel.

Nor was there a glimmer of that light when he stood in front of Iris, ending things, the night before Elspeth's return.

He'd contemplated sending Iris a letter, and even pictured the man on her route, Harv, delivering it, but letters left trails. They always turned up as evidence in the movies, and beyond that he wanted to behave as decently as was still possible. He stood near the door without taking his shoes off, and was aware of the fact that he kept rolling up on his toes the way his father did. It was a habit that had always annoyed him, and he wasn't sure when he'd made it his own. There was a mirror at the opposite side of the room, above the fireplace, and he saw his head pop up and drop down as he rolled. He looked ridiculous. He felt ridiculous.

"Are you coming in?" asked Iris.

"Well, I—" he let his voice fall, rich with meaning. "No. I'm afraid not."

Was that enough?

Did it make things clear?

His eyes darted around the room, taking in the ordinary things: a winter landscape hanging crooked on the wall; the door reflected in the mirror, and the glass knob glinting in the low light. He only had to grasp it and open the door, then take himself down the stairs and back outside and never, ever return. He waited for Iris to say something but she stayed unbearably quiet, and he was sure this was a tactic designed to make him more uncomfortable than he already was. What should he say? He might try to tell her the truth, stammering through it like good old King George. Everyone had revered George, who had so dutifully accepted a job he didn't want and was ill-prepared for when it was thrust upon him. And he had come through shining, a knock-kneed stutterer riddled with shame and insecurity, transformed into the King of England. Perhaps he'd had something to hide?

He thought of all the days he had chewed over the sentence *I'm leaving you,* and it seemed preposterous to him now that he'd ever had that idea about the only woman he had ever loved. So perhaps he could say just that: *I'm sorry, Iris, but Elspeth is the only woman I have ever loved.* Or simply: *This is goodbye.* That was corny, but there were occasions when corny really was the best way, such as that time so long ago when he had compared Elspeth's eyes to topaz. He felt sorry for Iris that even as he stood inside her home, Elspeth was foremost in his mind.

He glanced at Iris again. Her skin was shiny and her hair stood out in a frizz exacerbated by the humidity. Her pubic hair was just like the hair on her head, red and abundant, and it embarrassed him to know that about her—to know he would always know it when so few others did. She had put out a bowl of chips and placed a wine bottle in a Tupperware container of ice, just over there, where the fan was blowing, and those little gestures, the thought of her preparing for his arrival and squirting the perfume that still hung in the air, pinched his conscience. She was as predictable to him as he himself must be to Elspeth, and he wondered if love was always unbalanced, if indeed it had to be—or if the balance shifted back and forth over time. On his last visit Iris had called him gorgeous. He was definitely handsome next to her, whereas beside Elspeth he dipped below average. And he liked feeling good about himself. *Gorgeous,* she had said, and he felt it to be true.

Later there would be chocolates, he felt quite sure of it, because Iris loved to indulge, not just herself but him. (In his own defense he had done without chocolates for so long.) He felt a pull toward her, when he thought of being wanted, of drinking wine in the afternoon with a melting ice cube, of acting on impulse. She must have seen some change on his face, some moment of opportunity, because she stepped toward him and slipped her hands under his shirt. Soft arms wrapping around him, her body like a pillow or a cloud. Tongue invading.

Afterwards it seemed cruel that he still had his shoes on —or maybe it was just spontaneous, something he'd never really considered himself to be. He felt quite certain, as he lay on the sofa with Iris sleeping on top of him, that four times constituted an affair, and that the tenderness after the act, lying snuggled this way, was worse than the act itself. But what could he do? He owed it to Iris to stay put, at least for a little bit while she finished her sleep, though it did occur to him that she wasn't sleeping at all, and only wanted to keep him for that much longer. These were the subtle maneuvers women excelled at, and that had taken him the better part of four decades to recognize. A flicker of anger with that thought, just slightly. Could it be that Iris was using him just as much as he was using her? He had been coerced and manipulated all his life, as a soldier, as a husband whose chores got done before he could even get to them, and as a father who had not been able to insist on a second opinion for his daughter. *She isn't normal.* His eyes brimmed at the certainty. He had known what was best for his child, but he had acquiesced. He was the king of acquiescence, or the joker.

Again his gaze fell on the army picture of Iris, and he had the urge to wake her and tell her about those pathetic hours at Dieppe—the pebbles in his nose and mouth, the body on top of him, the weight just like now if he closed his eyes, and the warm, wet feeling of blood on his skin, not his own, but something he needed to atone for. He pulled himself out from under Iris and sat up, heaving to catch his breath, and then weeping into his hands. Huge, loud, unhinged sobs. And the fact that it was Iris comforting him only made him sob more, because of how good it felt, because of how much he longed to be held.

The words linking me with David were washed away by rain, and I tried to act as if they'd never existed. But in reality, the phrase was etched in my thoughts. And David himself was everywhere, even where he wasn't, meaning that any boy of a certain size and shape seen from a distance brought on that sense of dread in me. Whenever we saw the real him, Suzy would nudge me, and say, "Wonder if he loves you too." And then, "Teasing, Ruth, I'm teasing!"

One Saturday we were walking downtown, and Suzy

pulled me into a record shop and showed me the albums she wished she had. I saw him walk past the store as she was flipping through them, and felt grateful she didn't seem to have noticed him.

"This one especially," she whispered, pulling the album out and admiring the cover. She traced her finger over a red swirl at the top right-hand corner. "If it would fit under my top I'd take it right now." She giggled, and glanced at the clerk, but he was staring out the window eating popcorn. "It would fit under yours, Ruth."

"What?!"

"He'd never see it."

"No way!"

Suzy shrugged, still smiling. We wandered back outside, and I was glancing around for David when she asked me, "Ever steal before?"

"No—never! Of course not. Have you?"

Just as I remembered the chocolate bar, she said, "No. Never had the guts. But I bet it would be fun. Give you that zing, you know? And who would miss one silly album? I love every song on that album, every one." And she started singing.

So had she stolen or had she never stolen? Did she discount the chocolate bar because she'd been caught eating it? Or had she just forgotten about it? Or maybe she'd forgotten she'd told me, and she was ashamed, and didn't want me to think badly of her, which of course I never could. But what about the bees? Or the cat and Aunt Dodie and the kittens? Again the chilling sensation of looking at her and seeing a stranger.

"Look," said Suzy. "There's David." She waved.

He waved back, and glided towards us just as he had at the beach. I felt my face burning.

"Maybe he'll do it," she said, and paused as her gaze travelled up to mine. "I mean if you won't."

"Okay," I said, pulling at her sleeve. "Come on."

"You mean it?" Suzy clapped her hands and jumped up and down. "Listen, it's maybe better if I stay out here. You'll be less nervous without me."

It felt wrong that I was going into the store alone, to do something I didn't want to do, and leaving her outside with David approaching. But I went willingly. I couldn't look at David—maybe he'd be gone when I returned.

I walked in the store, I went right to the album she'd shown me, and I looked at the boy at the cash desk, who looked at me. He had seen me around school and town often enough to be unimpressed by my stature, and he quickly went back to his window and his popcorn, looking out on the day going by as if watching television. I saw my old friend Grace with the thick glasses pass the store window, and I thought to myself, if she turns and sees me, I won't do it. I absolutely won't. But Grace didn't turn, so the decision was out of my hands. I lifted the album out and slid it under my top. My stomach was sweaty and the cardboard stuck to me. Suzy was wrong, there was no "zing," only a queasiness. But Suzy was right too; you couldn't tell I had anything concealed. I thumbed through a row of albums, and left again. It amazed me how easy it was to break a law, just like breaking a rule, but bigger.

Outside, Suzy was sitting on the bicycle racks and David was still beside her, smoking a cigarette. He had eyes like opals, hard and pale, and he winked at me without smiling.

My heart thudded in my ears and my fingertips, and I looked away.

"So?" said Suzy. She brushed her cheek with the end of her ponytail. "Did you get it?"

I glanced around to be sure no one was watching, and lifted my shirt to show her the album.

Suzy laughed. "What! Why did you get *that* one?" She reached out and took it in her hands, and I felt it peel away from my stomach. Suzy recoiled, nearly dropping the record. "Yuck, Ruth! Why is it all wet?"

I grabbed it back and put it under my sweaty shirt again. David was laughing, and so was Suzy.

"You said to get that one—you *showed* it to me!" I thought of the red swirl, and her finger following it.

"Not that one—God, Ruth, I hate that band." She was still laughing, and she kept looking at David, whose laughs were like dumb grunts with big pauses between. "Just keep it for yourself, honestly," said Suzy. "Thanks though." Laughing still.

There I went, moving out of myself, moving way up so that I could look down on my pained expression, my big, ridiculous head hanging so my back hunched. Above me, a lamppost curled over as if mocking me. The lights of the convenience store's sign were buzzing and the florist was sweeping the walk in front of her shop. It was just the smallest, simplest moment when Suzy turned away from me, pretending she hadn't seen my face turn pink. David puffed his cigarette and blew a column of smoke at me. It travelled up like a vapour trail and filled my eyes so that tears formed.

"God," said David to Suzy. "Look at her shoes."

Suzy laughed again and said, "She has to have them

custom-made. Size seventeen! Right, Ruth?" Then she turned to David and put her hand out for his cigarette. "Can I have a drag?"

As she drew in the smoke, David tossed his head back and laughed again. "Look," he said, pointing at me. "I think she's crying—shit, is she your boyfriend, or what?"

Right then I understood that there are categories for love, the way there are languages within all language, and currencies of money. How stupid of me not to have known before. I opened my mouth to say something but couldn't think what it should be, so I closed it again. David laughed harder, with a hissing sound, and though it wasn't really he who had hurt me, I pictured myself reaching for him, wrapping my fingers around to the back of his skull and pressing my thumbs on his eyes, pushing into the sockets. Pushing and pushing. Maybe if I pushed hard enough the eyeballs would come out the back and I would have them in my palms, and they would be hard, not like opals but like marbles—nothing precious, parts of a game—and that would prove he wasn't human. I looked straight at him and sent him this thought: *So it is you not me there's something wrong with.* But his eyes were impenetrable, and Suzy was giggling.

I wanted to knock her down, so I turned and started running.

The record was still under my T-shirt, and I wrapped my arms around myself to hide it. My legs and my horrible feet carried the full weight of me along the sidewalk, past all the little people in my world, each with a little life of their own. Cars rolled by on the street, and the boy in the record store's window looked through me. The sweeping florist lifted her broom out of my way and smiled, and the fleeting kindness stung. I could feel my heart slamming against my chest wall. I ran on, wheezing. My toes pushed at the slits in my shoes and threatened to rip right through. A woman emerged from the bakery holding a birthday cake on one palm, and the man beside her held up his hands to stop me but I blazed by. I wanted to knock them all down, and I could have, just with a swish of my arm.

At the road's edge I stepped out without looking and slipped back to a day when Elspeth had let go of my hand. *Look both ways,* she had told me, and urged me forward to cross on my own. The wide world growing wider around me as I stepped carefully across.

How big I'd felt. How free.

Suzy stood in front of Officer McCaul, who'd been walking his beat nearby when the accident happened.

"I don't know why she started running," Suzy told him. Her cheeks looked feverish and her eyeballs danced. She twisted her hair around her finger. "I didn't know she stole the record either. I mean I wasn't with her. I didn't have anything to do with that."

"It's true, she didn't," said David. "I was with Suzy the whole time."

"Doing what?" asked the officer.

David shrugged. "Just talking."

"And then?"

David shifted from one foot to the other. "We were talking right there, by the bike rack, and then Ruth came out of the record store. Over to us."

"She showed us the record," said Suzy, talking fast now. "It was crazy, you were right across the street, and we asked her what on earth she was doing but—"

"Yeah," said David. "So when she saw you she ran—because of the record, I mean."

They looked at each other.

The officer, a young man who was new to the force, couldn't help feeling a puff of pride and imagining himself as he must have appeared in full uniform, striding along at such a pivotal moment. The precise stripe on his pant leg. The shine of his hard, black shoes. He had seen the girl running. They said she was seven feet tall. But before he could even raise his whistle to his mouth—if indeed that was what he was supposed to do—she was lying in the road, a truck was disappearing, and, in all directions, horns were blaring.

The boy who worked in the record store still had his bag of popcorn on the counter, unfinished. He had lost his appetite since the squeal of the truck's tires had forced him up off his stool, where he'd sat so long that his bum had begun to tingle. From the store window he saw the logging truck swerve, and a cluster of cars responding. But only when he got to the door did he see the body. The record sat propped against a sign post across the street, as if on display. At first he didn't realize it was a girl, lying there. But then he saw the strange shoes—huge things with heavy brown laces—and he knew who it was, and that she'd been in the shop moments before. Actually, he'd seen her both times. Once with the pretty girl, who was so much smaller, and then a little bit later, alone. He'd seen her put the record up inside her T-shirt, but he didn't like confrontation and he couldn't be bothered with petty thieves. Over the summer, he had been teaching himself to play guitar, and he'd had a revelation that music should be free, it should be everywhere, we should all be listening. In fact, at the moment of the accident, he was imagining himself bypassing the university he was headed to that September, and picturing his bookbag as a guitar slung over his shoulder. He would meander south, following the great arrow the geese made in the sky. And then the crash.

Later he heard she was seven feet, two inches, even taller than she looked. It occurred to him that if he had stopped her—if he had accused her of stealing—everything would have been different. That even the most peripheral person has a role to play. But to Officer McCaul he said little, for fear of the trouble he might get into, having assisted a thief. He only said, "Yeah, I think I saw her in the store this morning." And then, "No, I didn't realize she'd taken anything."

The woman who held the cake on her palm was named Martha, and the cake was for her twin boys, who were turning sixteen. Half the cake was chocolate and half white, to suit their different preferences.

After the accident, all of it lay splattered on the ground. No one had bumped Martha—not the giant girl running by, nor Martha's husband Bill, who'd held his arms up as she passed. Why he had done that, Martha didn't know, and it didn't occur to her to ask him until later, when they were lying in bed, reliving the scene.

"I don't know," he said. "She was just going so fast. Did you hear them say she's something like seven-foot-four? Shocking. I don't think I've ever seen that girl close up before. I guess I was just stunned and I had the feeling something was going to happen. Something bad. You know?"

"I know," said Martha. She smoothed the ruffles on her nightgown, and once again saw herself drop the cake as the tires squealed. "I've always felt that about her, just seeing her around town. She has tragedy written all over her, doesn't she?"

"Mmm," said Bill. "Some people do."

"Big, gloomy eyes. It was only a matter of time."

"Better, maybe, in the end."

"You mean if—"

"Mmm. Can you imagine a future for someone like her?"

"True enough. If she was a boy, it would be one thing. Big strapping lad. But such a huge girl. A *woman*." She grimaced and shook her head.

She kissed her husband's cheek, then, did up the top button of his pyjama shirt even though he didn't like it that way, and smoothed his chest the way you might smooth a packet you've finished wrapping. He switched off the light and they lay in silence for a while. She said in the darkness, "I heard the driver—that man Kowalski—he's got two little kids."

The florist had been hoping for a funeral. She sometimes did that, but never admitted it aloud, of course. It was never really an intentional hope, more a spontaneous one that came when there were too many flowers in the fridge and not enough customers. Unless someone died or got married, the

163

flowers would perish. Actually, they would perish regardless, but at least they wouldn't be wasted, and there would be money in the till. She had never been good at judging how much to buy. She loved all the varieties, and when the truck came around stuffed full with whatever was in season and reeking of nature's mingled perfumes, she was easily intoxicated, just as she was easily wooed by a man or by second and third helpings at dinnertime. But the business was suffering because of her whims.

As she swept the sidewalk in front of her shop, she was wondering two things simultaneously: how she could use up the old flowers in the fridge, growing transparent and wrinkly as the days wore on, and whether or not she could buy more before they were gone. She felt a sense of relief when she saw that the truck just crossing the bridge was indeed not her deliveryman, but rather Ned Kowalski heading for the pulp and paper mill with a load of wood.

When the giant girl ran by, she happened to look up just in time to catch her eye—a watery, blue, pathetic kind of eye that bulged like a fish's—and she was so struck by the girl's obvious distress that she smiled. It was only the smallest of gestures, like a door held open, but she understood the importance of such things. With her broom in her hand she stood watching the girl, lumbering and awkward, and only in that brief instant before the truck hit the girl did she open her mouth to gasp, knowing what she was about to witness. It happened so fast.

Later, she heard the girl was more than seven-and-a-half feet tall, and she thought, *I can believe it. I saw her up close.*

Ned had the radio blaring as he crossed the river with his heavy load, and he was thinking, *What a gorgeous day,* and looking forward to dumping his last logs at the mill, and then getting home to his family. He was building a set of stools in the garage, using a rich and grainy oak, and he had only today decided that he would under no circumstances stain them green in deference to his wife, who didn't know about wood but was a wonderful woman. If it were up to his wife, everything would be green, and green reminded him of bile and his mother's lumpy pea soup. As he sang along with the radio, he might have been driving ever so slightly too fast, because the music spurred him on and he wanted the day to be done. But he was a good driver; he was never reckless. He was thirty-two and he had never had a ticket. Once he had hit a buck but that had been ages ago. He'd been young, still an inexperienced driver, and it had been pitch black. The animal had stepped into the beam of his headlights, and there'd been no time to change course. In the seconds before the window smashed, he'd seen the bone of its antlers, and the eyes flashing, locking with his. It might have been this old happening drifting back that caused him to veer so swiftly when the girl stepped out in front of him. She must have been eight feet in height, arms and legs flying. The truck jackknifed, shooting across the bridge, smashing through the corroded railings, and landing, nose down, in the river. Inside, Ned was losing consciousness, with his head crammed against the steering wheel, gushing blood that was quickly diluted. He was spilling blood but filling with water, and he was dreaming of that other accident, when so many people had told him how lucky he'd been to survive.

Walking home, James went over the last hour with Iris, wincing with shame and wondering whether she understood it was over. He had been this close to telling her about Dieppe, but thanked God that he'd stopped himself just in time, and now he questioned why that would've been the ultimate betrayal. What on earth did war stories have to do with cheating on your wife, and why was it that his eyes always found that picture of Iris in uniform whenever he was entangled with her? What drew him to that? Before he left she'd caught him looking at the picture, and had come up behind him and rested her head against his back.

"That was the time of my life," she said. "Everything after was a disappointment. Until now."

He looked at her small, bright eyes, her hair pinned back in a style for a much younger woman. People opened themselves up for so much pain and sorrow. They stood right in the line of fire.

If there had been no war, there would be no such "time of my life." No such picture for reminiscing. But then if there had been no war, he would not have been with Iris, cheating on Elspeth, because he never would have married Elspeth in the first place. War had taken him to England. It had consumed Elspeth's parents and her brother Stanley and left her there in the shop, waiting for him. He felt a strange twist in his heart. What if Iris was the wife he would have had, had there been no war? And then he realized: if there had been no war, there would be no Ruth. And wasn't she his greatest gift as well as his greatest contribution?

He reached his house—a bunker with skylights and garden—and rushed toward shelter. As he grasped the door handle, he heard the phone ringing and ringing inside.

⚜

It was a perfect day for flying. Clear, for the most part, and blue. But Elspeth was anxious, and irritated by the fact that she had accidentally packed her book of crossword puzzles in with her checked luggage. Which perhaps was just as well, because on the flight over, unable to sleep, unwilling to converse with strangers, she'd worked on almost every puzzle, so that now there were only a handful of blanks here and there that would continue to confound her. Eventually, she'd flip to the back of the book and find the answers and pencil them in with the others, the loss of pride disguised by the sense of accomplishment and the neat letters filling each square. She hated to leave things unfinished.

Her row was called and she stood in the queue, thinking ahead to the delicious feeling of removing her shoes, sinking into her seat. There was a baby in front of her in line, a bright face peering over her mother's shoulder. Brown eyes wide, gold earrings gleaming in the baby's earlobes. Babies made Elspeth uncomfortable, but she smiled anyway. The child just stared, and seemed neither happy nor sad about Elspeth's presence but somehow surprised. *What are you doing here?* the baby's eyes asked. *What are you?* Elspeth looked away, glanced back, looked away.

When the line moved forward and onto the plane, she had the feeling of being pulled by the baby's gaze, as if an invisible beam linked them. Behind her, a man sighed heavily, his breath ruffling the hair on the back of her head, causing her scalp to prickle. An old fear was entering, blown in by a stranger. Fear of flying, or of falling; she couldn't quite name the uneasiness.

She had chosen a window seat, not because she wanted to look out, but because she had to, just to make sure nothing happened as the plane soared over land and sea. Rationally, she knew that she'd relinquished all control when she stepped on board, guided by a baby, but some vital part of her was certain of this need for vigilance, this belief that her very eyes on the open air would keep them aloft. Keep

169

all of them aloft, though in essence it was really herself she was concerned about—herself getting home to her family.

Elspeth fastened her seatbelt and felt a burst of relief at the satisfying click it made. People were still boarding, tucking their things into overhead compartments and squeezing past each other with mumbled apologies, but a quiet came over them when the plane eventually lifted off. Elspeth gripped the armrests. This second time flying felt worse than the first, more reckless. The more times you did something, the more chances there were for things to go wrong. She had a feeling of helplessness, from being up in the sky, at the pilot's and the atmosphere's mercy, and also from being so far from home, even as she drew closer. A certainty that something had happened in her absence persisted. Something that would not have happened if she had stayed, and the feeling reminded her of when she was a new mother and would periodically escape, alone, to do groceries or have her teeth cleaned. It was during her return home that she'd become most anxious, convinced that some disaster had occurred while she was away. Yet there they would be, James and Ruth, whole and safe, proving her wrong every time. She knew she had no gift for premonition, and that (in spite of the day of the strawberries) bad things didn't happen just because she wasn't there. Bad things could happen any time—but of course that wasn't a soothing thought.

Her thoughts travelled to a lazy summer day from her own childhood, when she was up in her room, looking down at her father working in the garden. Her mother, pregnant with Stanley, was behind her, making her bed, and glanced up in time to see Elspeth's feet disappearing from the window frame. Soft white curtains against a blue sky. Out she went, twirling. Her father with his spade, the homemade swing, the dirty brick house, and the neighbour's dog spun around her until her pink dress flew over her head. Then all there was was pink. Pink air on her skin. Pink wind in her ears. Pink light in her eyes. She landed in a swing made of arms, and her father looked down at her with his face drained of colour. This must have been the day her fear was born, though she couldn't remember feeling afraid. Above, her mother leaned out the window with her hands pressed to her mouth, and the clouds moved dizzily past her.

They were just like the clouds now surrounding the plane: gentle and puffy. Picture-book clouds that put her at ease. Somewhere below her was Cornwall, land of so many of the legendary giants and giant-killers she had read about on her hunt for stories with a happy ending. The Cornish giant Bolster could stand with each foot on hills six miles apart, and he stretched twelve miles into the sky. Looking down into the valley, he mooned over the pious and beautiful Agnes, a girl of normal size who had a lovely voice and would sing in the fields as she went about her chores. Bolster's lovesick moans and sighs could be heard over all of Cornwall, like a chorus to her song. Finally, the giant mustered his courage and approached her, stooping way, way down to proclaim his love.

"Will you marry me?" he asked.

Agnes studied the vast head, the great gapped teeth, and the eyes that were so far apart they looked in two directions. She had heard the giant ate girls like her, and here he was proposing marriage! But Agnes was a quick thinker.

"I will," she said, masking her revulsion. "Yes, I will, provided you prove your love by performing the following tasks."

She rhymed off races and duels and oodles of challenges, all of which Bolster completed with ease.

"Now?" he asked, wayward eyes blinking. "Now will you marry me?"

But Agnes insisted on one more task. She led him to the cliffs at the seaside and showed him a hole in the rock.

"If you fill this with your blood," she said, "I'll be yours forever."

From on high, Bolster peered down. His vision was not the best, but it appeared a narrow enough hole. It would be nothing for him. Right then and there he took a knife from his pocket, sliced open his arm, and let the blood spill. It poured out of him, but the hole didn't fill. Only in his last moment of life, when he had become so weak, so pale, and had crashed down with his face near the hole, did he hear the rush of water below, and see his blood draining into the sea.

The red stain still showed on the cliff there, but Elspeth couldn't see it from where she was. She flew up and over, and the stewardess handed out Lifesavers, the peppermint kind that James liked best. She fingered the package but didn't open it. She remembered that there was more to the Bolster story, as there was more to every story, depending on the angle of your approach: Bolster wooed Agnes, but was married to a giantess he had tired of. A great whale of a girl. For years he had ordered her to haul rocks from one place to another, and she had grown stooped and surly, as any woman would. Elspeth touched the wrinkles between her eyebrows, and folded her hands in her lap, where the Lifesavers rested, pure white rings. So who was the evil one? Agnes, who had been pious but unkind? Or Bolster, who had adored Agnes but mistreated his wife? And if you couldn't know who was bad and who was good, what was the point of the story?

She thought of a conversation she'd had with James about evil, back in the very early days when they'd talked about everything, at least a little bit, and how his take on the goodness of all people had made her less inclined to tell him more of what she knew—to spare him. Because it was somewhat charming, in those days, that he didn't believe in evil after all he must have seen and done. She didn't try to convince him of what she knew to be true: that evil was everywhere, that it spread like mould if you didn't viciously attack it, and that it was your moral obligation to do so. Or you would pay the price for having done nothing.

The day her parents had died, she'd sat in the sun among the strawberries, and a cloud had passed over—or something that caused a shadow. That was the moment she should have stood and run, the moment she knew what was coming. The hum came too, and then the sirens. But she sat still. Everything that followed hinged on those seconds of indecision. Later she hung on to the notion that everything happened for a reason. God's ways were mysterious, but not without purpose. What a crutch that had been so often through her life. Nothing had to be explained.

The plane shuddered and bumped, as though travelling over gravel, and an announcement was made about turbulence. The baby with the earrings was crying two rows ahead, and Elspeth gripped the armrests again. If the plane hurtled into the ocean right now, and everyone plunged to their deaths, she would still cling to idea of God's will as she descended. *This is happening because God wills it.* Or even, *This is my final payment.* But was that right or wrong?

The thought was as vast as the sky around her. A wave of nausea as the plane dipped and rocked. The plane shuddered again and a vision of the doctor came to mind. *There doesn't seem to be anything wrong.* Why had she always resisted a second opinion? Because it would be awkward to make demands? Or because of what might be found out? *The doctor knows,* she had said to James. *Doctors do. Do you have some fancy degree you haven't told me about? Why do you think you know more than he does?* She cringed, remembering. What he should have said was, *Because I know my daughter, that's why.* That's what Elspeth would have said if the tables had been turned, because Elspeth was smarter than James—and infinitely more foolish. He was far too good for her, and he didn't even know it.

How did anyone know anything?

And what could be more obvious than the fact that something was definitely wrong with their child?

She blinked and looked out the window so the person beside her wouldn't see she was crying. The clouds were like the mist at Niagara Falls, where James had taken her when she'd first come to Canada. The mist had been cold and relentless, but James had leaned into it and taken it like a gift while she had shrivelled beside him, shoulders hunched, eyebrows furrowed. The picture in her mind formed a portrait of their marriage, and she felt sorry.

Elspeth returned home smaller with a fine streak of white in her hair. The Lifesavers waited in her purse. As she walked toward Arrivals she worried that if she relaxed her muscles, her bones would shatter, and she would collapse and be unable to give James the Lifesavers. And what she needed to do most was give him something, and she knew he needed to receive.

He was waiting when she got there. She watched him through the glass doors and noticed how little he looked in his regular clothes, out of uniform, and how his longer hair, which she normally buzzed for him, stood straight up, as if saying hello to her. He looked sad and frightened, rumpled all over, and a thought flashed—*Something has happened to Ruth*—but was gone again. She put her hand to the glass and pushed, though his eyes had not yet found her.

No one spoke. A mechanical hiss and beep formed into a song with the ringing in my ears. I couldn't open my eyes, and yet I could see quite clearly. The smothering painted ceiling had no skylight, and I missed the glass roof of my room. How could I see the ceiling with my eyes sealed shut? I remembered wanting to press my great thumbs into the eye sockets of the boy David—how satisfying that would be—but perhaps it was my own eyes I'd pushed. Were they somewhere inside me? *How can I see with no eyes?* And then a transcendent feeling: *I can see without eyes.*

The ceiling split open and curled out to what looked like a black sky full of stars. I was travelling slowly toward them, and they were glowing brighter and brighter. But I was disoriented in such infinite space. I couldn't really be sure whether I was looking up or looking down. As I came closer, I saw. The stars were really only people, billions of sparks of light covering the earth. And there I was, falling toward them.

But then, giants were always falling. The great Finnish giant, Väinö Myllyrine, fell down his front steps one autumn, and found he could no longer walk. Over eight feet tall, nearly four hundred pounds, he was fifty-four years old at the time of his accident, and his joints were worn and fragile, like old, dry rubber bands.

As a young man, strangely handsome, he'd travelled through Europe, showing himself in suit, coat, and top hat. He almost made it to America, but his tour was cancelled because of the onset of the Second World War. War has a way of changing things. After it was over, he moved in with his mother. Their small house was surrounded by a dense hedge of fir trees that discouraged the curious, and behind it Väinö raised chickens, and tended apple trees, and sang in the sauna with his brother.

After his fall, his giant hip was nailed together again, but it never really healed. Väinö was transported from one hospital to another, but his condition deteriorated, and within months he died.

And don't forget the Texas giant, Jack Earle, whose father took him to Los Angeles when he was just thirteen, and paraded around town with him so he could get used to the fact people would stare at him. "Wherever you go," his father warned him, "people will always stare." The boy was already more than seven feet tall, and soon he was scooped up by the silent film industry, and found himself roaring without sound through *Jack and the Beanstalk*. One movie after another for years. But then one day he lost his footing on some scaffolding and hurtled to the ground during the making of a comedy that went on without him. The set shook when he landed, and a beam of wood crashed down on top of him.

The giant survived, and the miracle was two-fold, because after that he stopped growing.

—✦—

From the airport, James raced south across the border to a New York hospital.

"Why didn't they take her to the hospital at home?" Elspeth asked. Her voice vibrated strangely.

"No," James answered. "Too serious. She needs—" he hesitated—"special care." How could he explain that it wasn't because of the accident? He kept thinking of the word *macramé*, but that wasn't right, that wasn't it. Something *adenoma*. Since the moment of their reunion, he'd spoken in point form. The little words that connected things had floated away and he couldn't find them when he needed them, so he just pushed forward whatever would come and hoped that she'd be able to string the ideas together without too much distress.

"Where were you when it happened?"

He didn't answer. He didn't know if it was an accusation, and he didn't want to lie. But it wasn't the time for truth either.

"James, where were you, were you with her?"

179

With who?

He gripped the steering wheel hard but his palms were slick with sweat.

"Shopping," he said. "I was shopping." And he envisioned himself in the grocery store with a cart full of things that would get them through, keep them safe. *Reconnaissance missions,* those were called.

The guilt streamed from his eyes and made it hard to see, but he kept on driving, he kept on moving toward me with her at his side. They leaned forward, both of them, to get to me faster. All of the millions of obstacles disappeared as they raced along. And now there they were standing over me, one on each side, looking down. He was thinking, *What if I really had been shopping, and I had seen her run by? I might have stopped her,* and she was thinking, *I never should have left to take care of people who'd already died, when the living needed me.*

Even in my altered state I was the only one who understood the futility of constantly rearranging what was to what might have been. If this, if that, if not, what if, if only.

An X-ray showed a benign tumour—a macroadenoma—at the base of my brain, behind my eyes. The accident had lodged the tumour against the optic nerve, causing blindness. But long before that happened, the tumour's constant pressure on the pituitary gland caused the secretion of excess growth hormone, which for years made me grow rapidly taller. Finally an answer, but it only brought more questions. The plan was to shrink the tumour through doses of radiation, and thereby restore my sight and slow my growth.

Ideally, they would remove the tumour altogether; a minuscule sharp instrument would travel up my nostrils and into my skull, where the gland hung from the brain like fruit from a tree.

"But in your daughter's case it's just too risky now," the doctor told them.

A kind of whirring pause, like air leaving the room through a secret passageway.

"You should have come to us much sooner. Even with treatment she'll continue to grow for a number of years."

"And without?"

The doctor lifted his eyebrows. "Without? Well, there's no question." He shrugged. "She'll grow until her body can't sustain her anymore."

Elspeth and James waited, but the doctor cleared his throat and said nothing more. Hair curled from his ears and nostrils. He folded his fingers together and cracked his knuckles. Elspeth wore an azure suit with gold buttons, and kept her purse on her lap. James reached for her hand. Both James and Elspeth found some small comfort in the familiar face of the other. Together they turned back to the doctor and asked what more they should know.

"Her organs have been adversely affected," he said. "She grows, they grow." He held his hands up as though cupping a swollen heart. "She may well already be—let's say *dimwitted*. But that's a minor matter. Lots of 'normal' people are," he said, wiggling his fingers to convey quotation marks. He smiled, and then put on his grave expression again. "In any case, I must prepare you: even with the tumour removed, your daughter will not likely live a long life."

The doctor unfolded his fingers and stretched one empty

181

hand across the desk towards Elspeth and James as though offering something, but there was only an abundance of hair, and a ring too small for his finger. He pressed his palms together, like the praying hands mounted on wood on the wall at home. "This kind of thing is no one's fault," he said. "Nature errs now and again." Elspeth blinked and looked at the floor. *An error,* she thought. Somehow the news was not surprising, but rather a confirmation, or an explanation long sought.

Remembering this moment, I can feel the apprehension in her belly, her heart inside my own, thumping with fear, and James's longing to trust the man with eyes like holes in his face, doors you might enter if you were brave or foolish enough.

Much of that time in the hospital was like a dream. The night before my sight returned, I was sure that Suzy came to see me. She looked just like Grace when I pictured her, but I could feel Suzy's presence in the room, and smell a smell like apples and old cigarette smoke. I stayed as still as I could and waited for her to say something to me. And I was sure she sat down beside the bed and rested her head on my arm, and that it seemed like an apology. Her hair felt soft, and her breath on my skin was moist. *I'm sorry too,* I said. I said it quietly, just loud enough for her to hear, because what if you loved someone and then found out they didn't exist? Whose fault was it when the love could not possibly be returned?

In the morning she was gone, and when I opened my eyes, I squinted at the white walls the way you squint at snow on a bright day. I saw my foot protruding from the sheet, bare and pink. I wiggled my toe to be sure it was mine, though it could never be mistaken. At first the days and nights rolled together, but eventually I could tell them apart. The pattern gave me something to depend on.

Once I woke in the middle of the night to find Elspeth sobbing over me, and leaning to kiss my forehead. Her tears dropped on my eye, on the bridge of my nose. My face was wet with them. She grabbed my shoulders and pressed her face into my hair, crying, and everything turned the wrong way round, as with Suzy the night of Margaret's fall; Elspeth was a child waking from a nightmare, and looking to me for comfort, but I couldn't give what she asked of me, I didn't know what to do. I lay still and waited for her to go away again. In the morning, when she returned with James and sat by my bed, nothing was mentioned, and I noticed the shoes I had cut were gone and a new, larger pair sat in their place. And I felt thankful.

I understood there was a tumour, but my condition was otherwise nameless and mysterious to me. No one had labelled it, or explained in plain language what the implications were, or how such a thing could happen in real life, outside of storybooks. What did it mean for my future? The question was so terrifying that my mind kept travelling backward instead, finding a story I'd heard in kindergarten, about a "Giant S" from the Land of Oz. It had taken me so many listenings to hear the word as it really was: *giantess.* And Mrs. Yoop of Yoop Valley had been icy and cruel. When the Tin Woodman and his friends discovered her in her windowless castle of purple stone, she barely turned in her chair, where she sat eating buttered biscuits. The walls of her dining room were lined with plates of pure gold, and her immense body was covered in silver robes with floral designs. "Why don't you come in and allow the door to shut?" she asked them. "You're causing a draught, and I shall catch cold and sneeze. When I sneeze, I get cross, and when I get cross I'm liable to do something wicked." She was among the cleverest magic-workers in the world, and could transform anyone into anything. The very biscuits she ate had been mice just moments before, when a hankering struck her. She laughed when she told them that, and the expulsion caused such a breeze that the wobbly Scarecrow was almost blown off his feet and had to grab his tin friend to steady himself.

Was that what I was? A giantess? I couldn't bring myself to ask. But then on a bright afternoon as the leaves turned through the hospital windows, I was wheeled to a dark room, where a film reel clicked and popped, and a fairy-tale monster appeared on a screen—hunched back, protruding brow, prominent jaw, fleshy ears and lips. The film was about a woman who was twenty years older than me, and had what I had.

"It isn't as bad as you think," said the woman onscreen.

She had a spitty way of talking, and shiny, oily skin. Her thick tongue impeded her speech, and her voice was muffled, deep as a man's. She rested her head in her huge hand, and I saw her sausagey fingers, so revolting that I lost track of her words. I could see that she was kind, but that only made things more awful. I couldn't accept her existence as evidence that I would be all right because I saw, beyond everything else, the loneliness that ached all through her. It showed in her eyes, in the stiff way she held herself, in the beam of light that projected her onto the screen. The brightness that shone back at me felt as though it was pouring into me, and if I sat too long in front of it I would become just like her. But then she said, "It isn't your fault. It isn't anything you did that made you this way." She leaned forward and smiled, showing teeth with wide gaps. "You've got to use what's been given to you. That's the part you can control. That's the part that's up to you."

And as I sat staring, the light from the screen warmed me like sunshine. I believed I could feel the tumour inside me, a hot white stone trapped in one of the least accessible parts of the body. This was the thing that held the secret of my vast size, and now that it was known to me I felt a bewildering need to protect it, even as they shrank it away, as though it was me, myself, hiding there, and not the seed of all my problems. At the same time I loathed myself more than ever, and all that was wrong with me. The two things were inseparable: me and my condition. We were one and the same. I questioned every twitch and pain—the ringing in my ears that had for so long kept me awake late into the night, wondering what would become of me. I had a feeling of falling slowly, of never landing, my stomach collapsing as I spun through the air. Where once I had put one foot in front of the other and taken myself from place to place, now I had lost all control of my future.

When the film ended, I grew cold. I could not erase the image of the woman looking at me, talking to me, and the *tick-tick-tick* sound of the reel spinning and spinning, like a bomb, like a life running out. I wished I could move things back to the day of the accident, and never find out what was wrong with me, but then I pictured myself walking to school again, doing everything I had once done, and the sadness, the sameness, weighed on me. There I would be with the others and the little teachers, with my knees crammed beneath my already oversized desk. A gush of relief when I was allowed to stay home. A wish to say thank you, but an awareness that those words might give me away. So silence, always silence. Elspeth pulling my covers up under my chin, kissing my forehead. Closing me into a room that couldn't contain me, and waiting, just waiting, for another day that offered less than the one still passing.

Every day of my recovery, the Statue of Liberty stood guard, with her green copper skin and bones of iron. She could see into my window, and during the long nights when the hospital turned dark and quiet, she would sometimes dip down and whisper to me about all of her adventures. She had arisen in Paris, surrounded by scaffolding and getting taller and taller so that eventually she towered over rooftops and monuments and the tallest trees. She grew tall enough to learn a massive, wonderful secret: that there was no one in the firmament. It was only a vast, empty space that looked down on this one, seething and soaring with life. A space to contemplate what you should have done when you were there, waiting to get to heaven.

Her construction was so costly that once in a while a piece of her was packed up and shipped off for viewing. Her hand gripping its torch travelled without her all the way to Philadelphia to take part in the Centennial Exhibition. You could pay fifty cents to climb out to the lacy torch balcony. With the fair over, the lady's hand moved on to Madison Square, where it stood for years, like an old ruin that had lost its context. Eventually it crossed the ocean again, to join the rest. There, the lady's graceful head and shoulders were shown in a palace garden at the Paris World's Fair, and people lined up by the hundreds to go inside. Other parts of her appeared throughout the Champ-de-Mars park, but she was not truly spectacular until she was whole. She stood one hundred and eleven feet tall, from her heel to the top of her head. Her eyes were each two feet wide, her stern mouth was three.

But before long she was dismantled into hundreds of pieces, and sent in crates across the ocean. The warship that carried her rocked through a black storm. Her giant toes and fingers, her eyes peering through a slat, the salt water stinging. Upon arrival she was put together, and became something larger than life, a figure worth revering, though she wasn't human at all.

James and Elspeth came upon her as they walked the streets of New York City, looking dazed and foreign, dwarfed by their surroundings. He kept his hands in his pockets, and she linked her arm through his, which was the way they had walked when they were courting. How many moments are just echoes of earlier moments?

They boarded a train that plowed through the underground and surfaced now and again in the bright daylight. People scurried on and off, and rats dozed in the sewers. No one but Lady Liberty stared at James and Elspeth, because without me, there was nothing unusual about them.

Elspeth, having just come from London, noticed the busyness less, but to James it seemed there was not a spot on the pavement that stayed unoccupied for more than a

187

second or two. People swarmed the streets and left layers of invisible tracks. They passed in cars and on foot, by bicycle. They stood on street corners, wolfing down hot food from paper napkins. They teemed from buildings that stood storeys high, and you would think that in such a crowd, with so many sites to wander to, two people could lose themselves easily, but the lady always found them. From her little island, she beckoned them forward, and finally they squeezed onto the ferry and rode toward her. She really was colossal. She really did make your jaw drop when you stood at her base, looking up. James thought but did not right away say that her crown's windows reminded him of military pillboxes —places to shoot from. The clamour of war was in his ears again, just for a moment.

They climbed the spiral staircase to the crown, and when they looked out, they saw more people milling below. Separately, they were reminded of their honeymoon at Niagara Falls, and how being a tourist at such renowned destinations makes you feel small and pointless, but also part of something, and so less fearful of your insignificance. *It doesn't matter*, James thought, almost smiling, nearly lighthearted. *Nothing is the end of the world.*

It was up there, in the crown, that James pulled his hand from his pocket and squeezed Elspeth's fingers. He brought them to his mouth and kissed them—a rare, intimate gesture—and she looked at him as if he were crazy.

He turned and gazed through the pillbox window.

"I have something to tell you," he said.

It is August, 1942. The day before the ships pull out, James sits with two friends—Charlie and Gord—enjoying tea and scones. Tea tastes better in England, scalding and pure. He doesn't know why, but it does. Afterwards he'll think of this day often, the hot tea and his companions, especially Gord who says that when he gets home he wants to skinny dip with a girl named Joan. "In Tea Lake," he says, stirring his tea. She offered once—it was actually her idea!—and he turned her down. The lost moment is all he can think about this far from home, in a country swimming in tea.

James groans in commiseration. But at the time, to James, there is nothing special about the afternoon. It isn't until nighttime that they are told they'll be going on a manoeuvre, and the next day the trucks line up and man after man gets loaded in. They ride to the shipyards with the tarps tied down over top of them, and on board the troop carrier they are given their instructions and their ammunition, including two grenades. One by one they go out on deck to prime their grenades, because accidents happen—they happened on board other ships, when the men went out in groups, and one person's mistake means everyone around him goes down.

As the ship pulls away, James looks back on England getting smaller, and has a weird feeling of losing something, though England is not and never has been his home.

It doesn't take long to cross the Channel. It's dark as they approach France, the wee hours of the morning; this is meant to be a surprise attack. He can hear the water sloshing, and thinks it looks like thick, black oil. A vast sea of oil. They climb into the landing craft in silence and begin to rock forward over the waves, but suddenly flares of light rip the sky and illuminate everything. He sees more ships, more landing craft stuffed full with soldiers. He sees Gord's face, turning back to look at him. White like a moon. Another blaze of light and a ship in the distance is on fire. Still they move toward shore. The water explodes around them, great fountains shooting high, and as he leaves the boat, someone behind him—he can't see who—gets hit and plunges into the water. James feels hands grip his ankles and he begins to sink, but then the grip loosens and lets him go. Not a stranger but some man he knows, dying, just as James floats to the surface. All through the water there are bodies, already. On the beach there are soldiers in pieces. He's there with his rifle and his two grenades, his clothing drenched, and the enemy everywhere above and around them as the sun rises, but they're too far away to hit. He can hear and see the sniper fire coming in an endless stream, but he can't find a single man to shoot at. Only his fellow soldiers like a net around him. Everywhere they run, they trip over each other.

And the sound is deafening—the gunfire, the planes overhead, exploding and falling, the men screaming, the bombs whistling down. The tanks slip on the stony beach, undone by pebbles. Rocks spray up and fly like bullets. They ricochet off his helmet and graze his shoulder and he thinks for a moment he's been shot. He runs for cover behind a stalled tank and looks for someone he knows, someone who will tell him what to do now that nothing is going as planned, because he's useless without orders; he's been trained to follow orders. On the ship over, under the dark sky, Gord said this was just what would happen: that every battle passes in confusion, beginning with a plan that gets blown apart in the first few seconds of fighting. Where is Gord now, and Charlie? He can't think for the noise. There are people ablaze, trapped in curls of wire. A man catches his eye and mouths, *Shoot me.* He's bleeding from the neck. He won't live long. He's suffering. But James can't bring himself to do it. He looks away. He stays facing the other direction, but the man's gaze pierces his scalp. He can smell blood and shit and smoke and the salt of the ocean. A leg in a boot lies beside him. The beach is littered with bodies, with rifles belonging to the dead and wounded.

It seems like an eternity spent darting out, shooting at anything, finding cover again behind the sacred tank. He pulls the pins from his grenades and throws them, but he has no idea where they land. Smoke rises in columns of pink and orange, toxic black. He thinks he sees Gord running past with no helmet, and he calls to him, but his voice is lost.

Still, the idea of Gord makes him venture out again, though he can't find him. He trips over stones and guns and fellow soldiers, and falls to the ground as something whizzes past his ear. And then he's too far from the tank to risk going back. He lies there in his wet clothes, among the dead. There's a face right beside him, eyes open. The cuts on the cheek might be from a normal day. He hears another bullet enter the clothes and body of the young man, and sees the body rise and fall with impact, but there is no change on his face, which holds the look of shock, of terror. *If this was the last thing you saw in life.* James closes his eyes against the face. He grips the rocks and squeezes his fingers around them, and finds that he has lost his ability to stand. *Get up,* he tells himself. But he can't make himself go, he won't follow his own orders. He opens his eyes again and looks at the face, and then he reaches forward and shuts the eyes that accuse him. He grabs the man's arm and pulls—pulls and pulls until he's under the body. It might not protect him, but it might.

How much time passes then? He can't say. Six times he sees the same man going by, carrying wounded soldiers toward the water. He cradles them in his arms the way a mother holds a baby. When James dares to lift his head and look further he sees something white flying—a shirt or a hankie, it doesn't matter that it isn't a flag. Someone calls, "Every man for himself," and he pushes the dead man off and makes for the water, red now, in the daylight.

⚜

The redness returned her to the strawberries. She told him the story of that day. By now they were sitting on a bench near the statue, looking out at the water.

"I'll never forgive myself," she said, but wondered for the first time if she could, or might, now that there were new things to feel guilty about. "You were right," she said. "About the second opinion."

He looked at his feet beside hers, unsure how to answer. "Not right enough," he said finally. "I didn't push. But it won't help us to dwell on that now."

"No. But it needs to be said."

As they watched the ferry approaching he smiled at her and said, "Let's go see our girl."

They boarded with their arms linked, and their two stories together were like strands made into a knot; you cross them, you tuck one under the other, and cinch them closed.

So simple, and yet it took me forever to learn to tie laces. I thought I would never know, and then one day it came to me. I thought, *That's all?* Because it had looked so complicated for so long.

~✻~

There is an uncanny resemblance between real giants and giants in fairy tales. The Cyclopes giants of Greek mythology have one eye in the middle of their foreheads, and lousy vision, and in real life a tumour may well press on the optic nerve, skewing peripheral vision, or even causing blindness, as with me and Jack Earle.

A child giant shoots straight up, more or less proportionately, but if he manages to go through puberty—or if his tumour forms in adulthood—his height growth stops, and a new, more insidious growth begins. His skin turns thick and oily, and the bones of his hands and feet expand. His big lips and jutting chin, his swollen nose and ears—all of these changes happen because his soft tissues, like his organs, can't stop growing. The bony overgrowth in his face and nasal passages gives him earth-quaking snores and a deep, hoarse voice that scares children. His foul mood and his bouts of rage may be brought on by his frequent headaches, the pain in his joints, and the overall discomfort of a condition he cannot control.

He's nothing to fear, despite his immense size and his hunched back. An excess of salt makes his muscles swell with water, so he's huge, but he's actually weak. His big bones press on his nerves and make his arms and legs tingle. His bloated heart can't pump enough blood to serve him, and he tires easily, through no fault of his own. Often he carries a club—a tree ripped from the ground—because

193

his knees and ankles can't take the weight of him, and his feet have been squashed flat. The club is his cane—without it he cannot walk.

Only in fairy tales is he almost always a man. If he survives to the end of the story, he might be spotted disappearing over a mountain and down into a cave, in the wildest, least inhabited region. All too often that's where he goes to escape the civilized world, because if he lived within it, what would we make of him? And how would he see us, in turn?

My treatments were finished for a time, but I appeared the same on the outside. I returned home, and found a fat, hard-covered sketchbook waiting for me on my bed, with a set of pencils that came in a red tin container. I opened the book and smoothed the blank pages, but I couldn't think what to draw, and I was distracted by the world outside pressing in. The news about me—*the giantess*—had followed me home, so reporters popped up on the doorstep, wanting a look at me, and the telephone sent out shrill cries like a peacock screaming. The sound came at night too, as the three of us sat together in the living room playing Parcheesi. The dark spaces on the board were "safe spaces," but the house was a safe space too, we all felt it. It smelled of us; everything in it was familiar and held the prints of our fingers. Elspeth made popcorn and James scooped it up in handfuls as we ignored the telephone together, crunching away and chasing each other around the board and deciding, in unison but without words, that the questions on the other end of the line were no one's business but our own.

How old is she?
How tall is she?
How much does she eat?
How much does she weigh?
What size are her shoes?

I learned there was such a thing as the Tallest Living Woman in the World, but whoever she was would die, and someone else would be tallest until another soared past, crippled by weak bones and bloated organs, but phenomenal just the same. Even if her greatest goal was to grow vegetables. To this day I wonder, what if there was a title for most average? Or kindest? Kindest Living Woman in the World.

The house next door sat in quiet darkness, and the more I ignored it, the more it grew in the periphery, with the moon hanging above, and the dark windows, and the sense of emptiness all around. I knew it meant Suzy had gone. When I finally inched my way next door I brought my sketchbook with me. I had barely cracked open the book, only enough to smell the pages. I knew it held so much more promise than the notepads and loose sheets I had used forever, and I didn't want to spoil that by drawing the wrong thing, or by drawing something wrong. But now I knew what had to come first.

I looked through the windows of Suzy's house. The curtains on their clothespins had been left behind, but there was enough of a crack to show what remained inside—a stained mattress with the stuffing spilling out, and just beyond it, a doll's head, parted from the body. Nearby was a heap of everything: an old soup tin, toy trucks and cars, pantyhose, cereal boxes, a tube of toothpaste, and half of a game board. I had the sense that I had seen it all before. I sat on the grass and sketched the exterior with my big, clumsy hand shading everything grey, not a Suzy colour at all. Later I kept examining the drawing, and studying the real house too, expecting Suzy to part the curtains and look out at me in a burst of colour.

And then one day the colour appeared in a bouquet of flowers on the step. My first thought was that Suzy had died, and I ran out to our yard, looking for Elspeth, crying out to her, "What happened to Suzy?" and thinking, *Was it my fault?* But the flowers weren't for Suzy.

"They must be for Patrick," she said. "I don't know why they bothered," she added with a roll of her eyes. "Those people won't be back here again."

But people always came back, in one form or another. Elspeth knew and I knew too, though neither of us said it. I remembered how Suzy had once boasted that they'd moved thirteen times, and felt a glimmer of happiness that perhaps she hadn't lied about everything—perhaps there were other things that had been true.

"But what happened to Patrick?"

"Nothing happened to him. He's a little hero," said Elspeth, allowing a smile for the boy who looked something like Stanley. She was pinning clothes to the line—her own, James's, and mine—and they hung there like versions of us in the cold, fresh air.

I had known nothing about Ned Kowalski until then, but as the story unfolded, I saw Patrick, silent wisp of a boy, lurking by the garbage cans at the corner as I stood talking to David and Suzy.

He was watching us, the way he'd spied on us at the beach and maybe in all sorts of other places. When I ran, I ran right past him. The truck tires squealed and I fell, skin scraping against the pavement. Patrick was the first to get to me. He stood over me, wishing. My eyes were closed, and he held his breath until he saw the vein in my neck moving. I was alive. People pushed past him and crowded around me, and Patrick ran and jumped into the water, plunging down to the cab of the truck. The window was open and the cab was full of water, and Ned was crammed against the steering wheel. Like a fish, Patrick floated in. Finger by finger, he loosened Ned's grip on the wheel, then pushed and pushed with his hands and feet until the body was released into the river. They floated to the surface, as though something pulled them up. Patrick saw the sky beyond the waterline as he rose and burst through. There were others involved then—a fireman and the baker's wife and a bank teller—but it was Patrick Malone who'd saved a life. A fountain of water plumed out of Ned Kowalski, and it looked just like the stream a whale shoots forth. The man was breathing, and the little boy dripped a trail of water as he moved away from the scene.

It was a Friday when James veered from his postal route to visit Iris. *I never work Fridays,* he remembered her saying with a hint in her voice. *I'm always home Fridays.* True to her word, she was. She didn't let him in, though. She stood at the door with the chain on and peeked out at him with a grim eye. He muttered his apologies in the drab hallway, a light flickering above him. It would have to be good enough. He kept his voice low, in case the other apartments had ears, and when she didn't respond, when she didn't say anything

197

more than "Is that all?" he decided it would be wrong to ask her if she planned on telling anyone about their affair, namely Elspeth. They stood for a moment not saying anything, and he saw that she began to blink more rapidly. He put his hand through the crack to touch her shoulder, but Iris pushed the door against his fingers, and opened it only enough to allow him to slink off down the hallway, worrying his sore hand. He felt blood swimming up to a fingernail, and he was actually grateful for the wound. The carpet in the hallway was stained, he noticed, with years of traffic. A grey smudge discoloured the centre, and led off to each little home. He followed the main path and took himself outside, closing a chapter behind him.

Whether she would tell remained to be seen. Would *he* tell? he wondered, wandering home. He wasn't sure. Perhaps one day, but not now, and whether that was because he was cowardly or because it was just the wrong time to layer on pain and grief, he didn't know. He was less afraid of confessions than he had once been, but he better understood their complexity. If he confessed, it had to be for Elspeth's sake rather than to assuage his guilty conscience. It was she, more than he, who mattered. Unless of course you asked her. Then it was he, more than she.

She had returned to work at the factory, with red-haired Iris and the rest, minus Margaret. There were no swathes of fabric mysteriously slipped into Elspeth's bag these days, and Elspeth supposed she should have acknowledged the gifts at the time. At break, among the others, she took out her knitting and set to making a pair of socks from her left-over bits of wool, working the thickest strands into the toes and heels—James's socks always had holes there, where his skin shone bright and vulnerable, but he never complained. As the women chatted, the non-pattern spun out in rows of yellow, blue, red, grey, black, green. And in making something so wild, so at odds with herself, Elspeth often thought back to her father's toes after the first war—his heavy, damaged feet resting in her mother's lap while the radio sent out dramas in the evenings. *The Flowers Are Not For You to Pick.* That was one whose title had stayed with her, though she could no longer remember the storyline. Wasn't it amazing, she thought, that even in deepest winter, James's feet were always warm when they came up against hers beneath the covers? Night after night, his warmth radiated toward her.

Even now that I'm a grown woman, no one can really say for certain what will happen, or when, though chances are the oldest woman in the world will never be the tallest woman in the world, and vice versa. So for now I keep going, like anyone, moving through the years as long as the years will have me. Every summer I pick cherries and every fall I pick apples and every winter I tell schoolchildren what it's like to be me. Sometimes I ask them, "Well, what's it like to be you?" And they giggle and shrug, but I can see them thinking. My big body is only my container, I tell them, and my real self always looks out through the eyes.

Of my darkest and brightest days I don't say much, but I think of them often. Sometimes I step outside my yellow room, rise to my full height, and take a giant's view of those days, and the town with its snaking river, bridges arching over as in London, England. Straight across from the school with its bell clanging is the factory, where most of the baker's goods get eaten by the working women. The socks are here too, getting longer and louder at each coffee break. Out on the street, the man who will wear them delivers the mail as the man on the back of the garbage truck rides past him. Each nods to the other. Logging trucks move in two directions past the shops and the angle parking and two thick tree trunks, like the legs of a giantess. The florist sweeps her walk, daydreaming. And then, there I am, soaring by on my bicycle.

It thrills me to see myself so happy, with all of my future still ahead of me, however short or long it might be. There is no yellow string around my handlebars. It was dirty and frayed and had served its purpose. I look like a normal girl as I coast along, hair flying. A girl who loves bicycles and wind and the smudge of pencil-grey on paper. If I had to be known for anything, it would be those three things. People are always less and more than they seem. The Finnish giant grafted apple trees, and the Texas giant wrote poems, and the Willow Bunch giant lifted but also loved horses. The Missouri giant, Ella Ewing, was somehow radiant with her sticking-out ears and her bun on the top of her head. She liked to read and embroider, could play guitar and milk a cow, make butter, ride horseback, and hunt eggs, though not all at the same time. She was human, after all. A part of the ordinary world.

When I was small, the ordinary world was a land of giants. Everywhere I went there were tree-trunk legs and voices calling, *Hello, down there!* I remember watching my mother eat toast in great half-circle bites, and asking her, "Mum, do mouths grow?"—certain mine would never be so huge. I stretched my arm up to hold my mother's hand and took three steps for every one of hers, looking down at her long, narrow feet in black shoes. I stood against the door-jamb while my father measured me and marked the spot I had reached, each increase a cause for celebration until the day he refused to measure. My mother scrubbed the lines away, then my father painted over the faint remnants. I kept returning to that spot, staring at the blank space for any evidence that might shine through to me. What was it like to be so small? The loose exhilaration as my father slipped his hands under my armpits and swooped me up to the dizzying sky. And then I was riding on his shoulders, with my mother's careful hand around my ankle. I remember that. The powerful feeling of being raised so high that I could see further than those who lifted me.

Acknowledgements

It's hard to say where an idea begins, but one early inspiration for this story came from the Diane Arbus photograph, *Jewish Giant at Home With His Parents in the Bronx, N.Y., 1970*. Eddie Carmel stands in stark contrast not just to his mother and father but to the lampshades with their plastic covers, and the pleated curtains, and the chair covered by a wrinkled throw. The mundane scene is utterly transformed—and also illuminated—by the presence of the giant.

Over the years I spent creating Ruth, an entirely fictional character, I learned about many other people who'd grown to great heights, and whose stories helped me imagine what it must be like to have such a striking physical difference. My thanks to Jenny Carchman for the National Public Radio documentary about Eddie Carmel, *The Jewish Giant;* to Bette J. Wiley for *Our Miss Ella,* the story of Ella Ewing; Dan Brannan for *Boy Giant: The Story of Robert Wadlow The World's Tallest Man*; and John Kleiman for *Cast a Giant Shadow: The Inspirational Life Story of Sandy Allen.* I am also grateful to Kalervo Myllyrinne and Ovila Lespérance for making the stories of their respective uncles, Finnish giant Väinö Myllyrinne and Saskatchewan "Willow Bunch Giant" Edouard Beaupré, available online.

Though I have played with the details, the account of Anna Swan's escape from the burning museum comes from the *New York Tribune,* July 14, 1865. The advertisement describing Charles Byrne on view is taken from Edward J. Wood's *Giants and Dwarfs. The Giant Who Had No Heart in His Body* is my retelling of the Norwegian fairy tale collected by Asbjørnsen and Moe. The line about Gog and Magog "set forth in all their ugliness" comes from George Puttenham's *The Arte of English Poesie,* and the idea of Ruth "opening out like the largest telescope that ever was" and finding her rapid growth "curiouser and curiouser" pays homage to Lewis Carroll's *Alice in Wonderland.* The giantess Mrs. Yoop is directly quoted from L. Frank Baum's *The Tin Woodman of Oz.* The book's closing was inspired by a quote from John of Salisbury: "Bernard of Chartres used to say that we are like dwarfs on the shoulders of giants, so that we can see more than they, and things at a greater distance, not by virtue of any sharpness of sight on our part, or any physical distinction, but because we are carried high and raised up by their giant size."

Thanks to Hugh Cook, Julie Trimingham, Heidi den Hartog, Samantha Haywood, and finally my editor Robyn Read, for being such insightful readers. And to my husband Jeff for all our rich discussions about Ruth and the triangle of mother, father, and child.

The writing of this book was generously supported by the Canada Council, the Ontario Arts Council, and the Toronto Arts Council.

¶

This book was typeset in Bell MT which was originally cut by Richard Austin in London in 1788, and Adobe Caslon which was drawn by Carol Twombly in 1989.